I0457060

Journeys And Wizardry

Mary Catelli

Published by Wizard's Wood Press, 2016.

Thief, Thief!

The nests looked vaguely like the nests of several eagles, clustered around the cave, only much bigger. Though of course they would be larger. No dragon could fit in an eagle's nest.

Sylvie contemplated the pale dried brushwood of the nest as she walked up the road. These dragons did not keep the enormous piles of treasure a wyrm would demand, but she could see things through the brush now: a sapphire necklace hung from one branch; a broken chest spilled not gold pieces but pure white pearls; a tapestry of a dragon in flight hung between two boughs.

Sylvie walked right by. The dragons were not the lords of the land for nothing. She couldn't sell these things within the dragons' lands. They might be benevolent, held by their subjects and by travelers through the lands to be the most benevolent lords in many days' journey, but they were definitely dragons, with a dragon's memory. One of those pearls would bring unending pursuit, and no one would buy that pursuit from her.

"But if they only have some *books*," she muttered. Most potent magicians, the dragons were, and if Sylvie could find their books of magic, she could sell them. Any magician would give his right arm for those books, and could handle the pursuit as well. And Sylvie would be set for life.

She hurried quickly through the first nest. The wand with silver patterns might be magical, but it was human-sized and would be human magic. Only dragon magic would do. Besides, the dragons were seen flying off, but they would be flying back soon enough.

It was in the next nest that Sylvie found the first of the spheres: pale pink, perfectly spherical, warm to the touch, almost as large as Sylvie was. "An egg? But it's not egg-shaped." She glanced over the clothes and jewelry and went on to the next nest. Odd spheres buttered no parsnips.

There were half a dozen of the spheres in this nest and that one, but no books. Sylvie even looked through all the chests of gold and gems, disturbing them so that the dragons could see she had been there. She sat with a sign in the largest of the nests, half looking at the sky blue sphere in it.

"Well, it might be an egg, egg-shaped or not. But it might be a secret hiding place. I'll just tap it (she picked up a stick) and see if it's hollow. If it isn't, I'd best be off and seek my fortune elsewhere." Sylvie scrambled over the brambles and up to the sphere. Though she knocked softly at it, she could clearly hear the solid sound. Sylvie sighed and dropped the stick; then her practicality reasserted itself, and she began to leave the nest.

"Dragon eggs are round all over," she noted, climbing down. "That fact might be worth a few coins to some scholars—enough for a dinner at any rate."

Tap, tap. Sylvie looked behind herself. The blue egg shifted a little, and another tap shifted away a piece of the egg. A large bronze eye peeked out of the hole, looking directly at Sylvie, and an indistinct noise came from within the shell. Bits of shell flew in an explosion. A baby dragon, pale blue with enormous bronze eyes, leapt from the shell to run to Sylvie. "Mommy, Mommy!" Half-opened wings flapped widely as it tossed its arms about her waist and looked up at her adoringly. "Mommy!"

Sylvie gasped for breath. After a minute, she managed to persuade the baby to let go, but it curled up at her feet, closing only one eye.

Well, the dragons would not be pleased at this outcome. She could only flee and hope that they never figured out she had snuck into their nest. Sylvie started down the road. The baby dragon eagerly scrambled after her.

She turned to scold it when some thing moved over the sun. It might have been a cloud. Somehow, Sylvie knew it was not. She slowly turned to face the descending dragons. Her teeth worried her lower lip. There were seven of them; the leader was a pale golden dragon with silver and copper patterns running through its scales.

"WHAT?!? My love, my own, my darling Azurine has hatched! Where is he? What could have befallen him? Oh I should have known to not trust that spell that Eglatinor gave me! My darling chick has hatched without me, for all his promises! Where can he be?"

The pale green dragon who landed nearest to the road stretched a long claw. "There he is," it said slowly, and blinked.

The distraught dragon looked at the road. "A human? What are you doing here, human? And what have you done to my darling Azurine?" demanded the dragon, looming over Sylvie and Azurine.

"Help! Mommy! Save me!" Azurine dived behind Sylvie, his tail whipping around her feet, his arms around her waist, and one fearful eye peeking from behind her back.

"He *imprinted*," hissed a large black-bronze dragon. A murmur of hisses echoed through the nest. At least, Sylvie thought it was a murmur; still, had it been any louder, it would have deafened her. Azurine's arms tightened about her.

A smaller dragon, deep heart's-blood red, looked Sylvie over. "Well, she'll have to raise him now. It's going to be a bother, arranging for shelter and all—but you know as well as I, Auream, that we have no choice."

Sylvie stiffened. How long did it take a dragon to grow up? She glanced back at Azurine, trying to guess; he looked back at her with guileless eyes.

Auream gave a long sigh, smoke flowing from her mouth like fog. "There's no help for it then. We will have to arrange matters for this human." She settled down in her nest.

"But, Great Ones, I can not remain here," Sylvie began pitifully.

Twenty eyes looked at her.

"I make my living seeking out new magic, and selling it to magicians—I would surely starve, after."

Auream drew herself up on her hind legs. "New magic? Why, we have magics older than any civilization. We will give you new magic to sell to these magicians."

Sylvie smiled.

"Why, I will teach you alongside Azurine! He shall learn nothing that you shall not; I shall even test you as Azurine will be tested! . . . . Dear cousin Gillais, are humans *supposed* to turn green?"

Lifestone

"The Scarlet Citadel indeed," Richard said, looking up at the gray rocks looming overhead, stark against the brilliantly blue sky. "Wonder where they got that name."

Jonathan drew a deep breath, stepping up on the rocky shelf beside the other knight. "The Wizard of the Scarlet Citadel is certainly enough to drain life out of any place." He squared his shoulders and looked at the narrow crack they were heading up. The cliff face was as barren as a desert, without even a loose rock. "The wizard's got to be around here somewhere."

Richard glanced at him. "We are drawing near his stronghold. We should be more cautious; he will be strongest here." His voice slowed. "Perhaps we should even go back—tell the rest of the order that we caught him gathering forbidden herbs."

"We already wounded him," Jonathan pointed out and started up the track, "and consumed most of his spell-craft that he had prepared. Anyone who comes after will give him time to prepare again." His voice took up briskly. "Master Frederick would be ashamed of you; the first principle of fighting a wizard is to always remember that it takes him longer to strike a blow than it takes you."

Richard grimaced and followed him. "The chief point to remember in fighting a wizard is that you should fight to win, by whatever means will bring you victory. If we die, no one will know what the wizard was up to."

Jonathan started up the cliff; Richard sighed and came after. "You're going to get us both killed one of these days," he observed, casually.

Silence fell as the young knights saved their breath for climbing. A sharp breeze blew up the mountain; Jonathan looked down, and grimaced at the thought of the height. He turned his attention ahead, reminding himself that there was no telling what the wizard of the Scarlet Citadel was up to; he and Richard had kept the wizard from getting the deathberry he was after, but that could have been needed for one specific spell.

He looked ahead. The citadel was not far ahead, and it looked as if the cliff face turned into a brief flat area, just before the walls. He tried to see if the wizard had any surprises waiting for them there.

"You fools!" The wizard suddenly loomed out of the rocks ahead of them, his white hair and beard wild, his eyes fervid, his lips pulled back from his teeth. Something dark and red glittered in his hand like a sword.

Jonathan drew his sword and leapt to the attack. The wizard's crimson robes still carried the stain of blood, and the wizard himself moved stiffly. Jonathan's sword swept up to parry the wizard's blow, and a bitter, unearthly sound echoed. A glance showed Jonathan that the sword was unharmed, but he resolved not to let that enchantment touch his flesh.

Richard's sword flashed beside him, and Jonathan jumped to one side, up to the plain. The wizard snarled and fell back; his hands flashed, too quickly to be seen, and something shimmered in the air before him. He put out his free hand, and found it colliding with a slick wall of glass.

The wizard laughed, his thin body shaking. "Come and join me, you knights! Nothing but glass bars your way!"

Jonathan took a step back; he looked about, but there were no loose stones here, either. Richard stood to one side, his sword still in hand, but his expression was resigned. "We've got to go back," he said, his voice low.

Jonathan started to put up his sword. This would, indeed, take more knights from their order.

The wizard went on laughing. "You fools! You fools! To challenge the Wizard of the Scarlet Citadel!"

Something moved against the walls, behind the wizard. Jonathan frowned, realizing the movement was near a small door. The wizard noticed his attention and, breaking off his laughter, looked over his shoulder. A hideous smile broke on his face. Jonathan and Richard looked at each other, and back at the wizard, needing to know what he was up to.

A pale, thin woman cowered against the wall. The wizard's hand flashed out to fasten on her shoulder. "How convenient you are," he purred, and dragged her out into the open. Her brown eyes looked through the glass wall at the knights, but her face showed no further animation. The wizard pulled a sullen red stone out of his pocket and held it up; the gemstone glittered a little in the sunlight. "Watch what you have done, you fools, so proud of having harmed me!" He lowered the gem towards the woman. She shuddered, but did not try to pull away.

The gemstone touched her shoulder. His hand folded over it. "Watch what my Lifestone does for me, you fools!"

Red light began to pulse through his fingers, steady as a heartbeat. Jonathan took an involuntary step towards him. Blood seeped through the woman's thin dress. She shuddered, her eyes closing. The Lifestone glowed more, and the blood drew back from the cloth, towards the stone.

The knights watched in horror. Richard moved closer to Jonathan and whispered, "We have to warn the order, get someone up here who can deal with him."

Jonathan could not bring himself to move, or speak, or even look away. Minutes ticked by, and the wizard's robes no longer stuck to a wound; he did not withdraw his hand. His cheeks flushed with rosy color, and exhaustion flowed from his face. The woman started to slump, and the wizard did not hold her up, but he did not take his hand from her shoulder as she fell to her knees. Her eyes opened and looked blankly at the young men. Jonathan found that his breath was harsh and shallow.

He looked at the sunlight glinting off the wall, the only sign of its presence. He drew a deep breath, unable to remember more that one bit of lore: go straight through a broken window, without hesitation, and it would not cut. He backed up.

"What are you doing, Jonathan?" Richard whispered. He looked at the woman. "We've got to get out of here, to get help."

"Trust me," Jonathan said, through stiff lips. He drew a deep breath and broke into a run. A second before he collided with the wall, he shut his eyes.

The wall shattered, an enormous sound, all around him. Slivers cascaded over each other and chimed; they brushed against his face and clothing, but he felt no cuts as he fell forward. He opened his eyes and saw the scraps of glass surrounding him. He hurried to his feet, glad of the armor that would protect him from more than swords.

Richard shouted with glee and came running. The woman, pale as bone, did not even stir, and the wizard stared blankly. Jonathan went for his sword.

The wizard dropped the Lifestone and started gabbling. Jonathan and Richard reached him, their swords flying and cutting through the wizard's robes; blood spurted from his arms, but not before he pronounced the last word.

The door of the citadel creaked open, and an armored statue came out, every joint creaking as it approached them. Jonathan stopped by the woman, knowing Richard was right: they had no idea what wizard's preparations were within his own stronghold, and they did have to warn the rest of the order. The wizard scrambled back, and Jonathan dived for the Lifestone; whatever else happened, the wizard would not get that back. His arm went around the woman as he shoved the Lifestone in his pocket.

"Let's go, Richard," he said, glancing down the mountain. The statue took up position before the wizard, protectively, but came no closer.

Richard nodded, put up his sword, and said, "I'll carry her; you guard our backs."

The wizard limped inside the citadel. The woman did not seem even to notice as Richard hefted her to one shoulder and started down the trail. Jonathan shoved the Lifestone deep in his pocket, and followed after, keeping one wary eye on the trail.

Jonathan stood against the white-washed wall in the infirmary, his eyes flitting nervously about the room; Richard stood next to him, as anxious. The cause of their anxiety, Selina, mistress of the Keep of the Gryphon, sat gravely beside the sickbed, her yellow and silver robes bearing the symbols of her rank. The doctor, Althea, ignored Selina and fussed over her lily-pale patient; Jonathan wondered how she managed it.

"You are the woman Pearl whom Richard and Jonathan here rescued from the wizard of the Scarlet Citadel?" Selina asked gravely.

Weakly, Pearl nodded.

Selina inclined her head. "This order is dedicated to the purpose of bringing justice to these lands. I wish you to tell us of the wizard, and what manner of man he is."

"He is very wicked." Pearl stopped. A minute later, she gathered her strength again. "He has a thing, a Lifestone." She gestured, vaguely. "It drains life from one person to another; he drains the people of the citadel, to death." Her eyes moved to Jonathan, to Richard. "Even when he is not injured, he uses it, to keep his youth." She fell silent, not taking her eyes from the young men. "I saw you."

Jonathan shifted his weight uncomfortably. Pearl drew up her strength again. "I saw you and knew that someone had to know what he did. So I came out of the citadel. I knew he could not resist the temptation of health, so close to hand."

Jonathan looked at Richard; the other young knight looked as pale and shocked as he felt.

Even Selina looked a little paler. "I thank you," she said formally. "What you did shall not be in vain. We shall drive this evil from our land." She rose to her feet. "I pledge to you that the wizard of the Scarlet Citadel has claimed his last victim."

Pearl nodded. Her eyes closed. Selina glanced at the young men and started from the room; Richard and Jonathan followed.

Althea came as far as the door. "Ah, Mistress Selina?"

The other woman turned, tilting her head to one side.

Althea lowered her voice. "The wizard's last victim may be here. I do not think that Pearl will live."

Jonathan swayed, his hand going out to the wall for support. Selina looked sharply at him and Richard. "We are going to assail the Scarlet Citadel immediately, before you have time to rest. Therefore you will not be one of the force."

Jonathan bobbed his head obediently.

"Eat and rest, then." The woman turned and swept off briskly toward the armory.

Jonathan and Richard looked at each other. "The kitchens?" Jonathan proposed. Richard nodded, and the young knights started off.

Half a dozen knights were still sitting around the table, eating meals that duty had deferred. They nodded to the young men as Jonathan and Richard sat, murmuring something about their work; the rumors must be flying, Jonathan thought. He sliced off a piece of bread and spread butter on it.

A plump and scholarly knight came and sat by them. "I have heard of what you brought back from the Scarlet Citadel," Timothy began. He gestured. "The Lifestone?"

Jonathan thought of Pearl, lying in the infirmary. "Deathstone would be a better name for it," he said. "A piece of diabolerie!"

Timothy looked shocked at this error in his field of knowledge. "It is not diabolerie; it involved no demonic work. Nor it is specifically evil."

Jonathan slammed down the bread on the table. "That's impossible!" he protested. "To what good uses could it be put?"

Timothy looked abashed. "I do not know," he said, carefully, putting the tips of his fingers together. "Yet, when I tested it, it did not register as black magic."

"Easy, Jonathan," Richard urged. Jonathan's shoulders slumped, and he nodded. Richard turned to Timothy. "The wizard got the better of us." His mouth twisted. "Mistress Selina may defeat him, but he defeated us. The woman we tried to rescue is dying. The Lifestone killed her."

Timothy nodded, murmuring about what a tragedy such a death was, and how distressing a good knight found his first failure. Jonathan dished himself up some soup and stared moodily into it. Pearl was dying, in spite of everything.

He thought about the Lifestone again. A gemstone that drained life from someone, and gave it to someone else. . . he turned abruptly to Timothy. "Have you found out much else about the Lifestone?" The other knight looked up from his soup. "Need the stone kill its victim?"

Timothy shook his head. "No, it takes minutes for the gem to do that. It must drain much life to kill."

Jonathan nodded. A minute later, he excused himself and hurried off into the keep. Richard looked curiously after him, but Jonathan did not dare stop for his friend as he hunted down the storeroom where all magical things were kept, and the Lifestone.

It shone a sullen crimson again in the torchlight. Jonathan drew a deep breath, picked it up, and hurried out of the room, towards the infirmary. A stone to give life to another—a Lifestone, indeed.

Althea was gone from the room; Pearl slept on, her face still and pale as a lily. Jonathan sat on the bed, and she stirred a little, but did not wake. Jonathan took one of her hands in his, pulled out the Lifestone, and lay it between her hand and his shoulder. It began to glow.

Pain knifed into his shoulder. Jonathan's teeth sunk into his lip as he fought against crying out. His free hand reached out to take her other hand. "Even braver than I realized, to endure this." Pearl murmured a little, and he said, soothingly, "It's all right, you're getting better."

The Lifestone pulsed like a heartbeat. The agony spread, dragging itself from every limb. Color began to flush Pearl's cheeks, and she stirred. "What?" she said, bewildered.

"It's all right," Jonathan assured her, though he was beginning to feel faint. Her eyes fluttered open and looked at the scene before her. Comprehension flooded them. With a violent cry, she jerked her hand away from his shoulder, sending the Lifestone flying. "What...what did you think you were doing?" she demanded.

Jonathan dropped his free hand to the be, to hold him up, but did not release her hand. With the pain gone, the drain did not seem so great, but Pearl's cheeks were still rosy. "I counted on your taking only as much as you needed, refusing to take my life." He smiled. "There was enough for both of us." He yawned, leaned forward, and slid into sleep on the bed beside her.

Pearl looked at him for a long minute, but his color was good, his breathing deep and regular. She yawned herself and fell asleep, her hand still linked with his.

The Turtle in the Sea of Sand

The sea of sand touched many shores—the meanest beggar's brat knew that—and many sands drifted up from them, but Persinette always maintained that black sand meant death, and mingled with red, a bloody death. Kyre jeered at that: as if someone wasn't always dying in the city, and most of the time, dying violently.

Still, his heart jumped when he came out in the gray of morning, and the black and red lay tangled in the port, beneath the eggshell sky of morning. Around them spread the dips and rises of tan, touched with yellow and brown, that usually filled the harbor, but the red and black lay like the wake of a boat. He watched only a moment before he walked down the shore, staff in hand, looking for work. Violent death always lurked, but so did starvation, and the latter took longer. He scouted along the docks, where the merchants moored. Many a man had started unloading before the sky had even turned charcoal gray, but the longshoremen were men, and solidly built. A youth, and one small for his age, had no hope for work there. Kyre walked through the crowds of plainly clad vendors, sailors, and artisans; he glanced at the brightly dressed, but every time, the man was about his business and would hire no one now.

His eyes narrowed when he reached the smaller boats, where the young and well-to-do sailed for pleasure. Errands on the other hand, or messages, he could do—or better yet, guiding through the city, or his height was enough to guard a boat. He tapped his staff against the wood of the docks. Better pickings here than with the merchant ships.

Kyre appraised the boats. Rich young wizards arrived, full of exclamations on how strange the sea of sand was, and how the magics on it must work. He did not have to listen to receive his pay, and that they expected *water* in a sea did not keep them from paying well.

Sand hissed in the sea, the small dunes approaching the shore and falling back. A couple of the boats had not been there yesterday. Kyre walked toward them.

"You!" A shout came from one. Sand had not even started to gather in its windward side—a new ship. The only sailor, wearing fine greens and gold, stood with one foot on the gangplank. "You, in the blue vest."

Kyre's vest had been blue, once, and looked blue in the drab crowd of the docks. He hurried through the crowd, before anyone else offered to do the job instead, and better, and eyed the sailor: a young man, and if the clothing had not shouted his birth to the four winds, his lean hands bore no calluses. Kyre checked again. Except on his index finger, from the pen. Though he didn't look too pale, Kyre conceded. He must not shut himself in his study.

"I need someone to guard my boat."

Kyre straightened, looking bright-eyed and attentive. Old Anzar had taught him a few tricks with his staff and, if it came to that, with his knife. He could guard a boat.

"A silver star, and a copper bit for each hour."

Kyre did not move. A copper bit an hour was generous in itself.

The man looked at his face and paused. "And a second silver star if you have to watch until nightfall."

Far, far, far too much—but a dozen folk must have seen him get the offer. If someone else took it, he would be scorned the length of the docks as a coward and fool. He might never work again. "Anything about the boat I should know?"

The man grinned. "Not much." He stepped aside and bowed Kyre to the gangplank. Kyre walked up. The boat was small, and held only a few chests besides the sails. "A poor thing but my own," said the man.

Kyre looked at one of the chests: black, bound with iron, and nondescript, but he had not survived long on the docks by not trusting his instincts.

The man laughed. "I see your prudence is sufficient to the task. That chest is enchanted, but will harm neither you nor any other." He swept Kyre another bow. "Here is the silver star—the first."

Kyre bobbed his head and took it. Another wizard, more foolish than most. Kyre hoped he found the sea of sand fascinating.

Persinette, her hands filled with the charms she peddled, her lined face thoughtful, appraised the boat. "Who's the owner?"

Kyre shrugged. "Didn't ask." When Persinette lifted her eyebrows, he shrugged again. "So he doesn't pay me. Think I'd go to court over it? You got to pay the judge."

Persinette snorted and hobbled off. Then, thought Kyre, no wizard would buy her charms, and she needed to sell them. He sat back, not feeling the confidence that he showed Persinette. The coin seemed to burn in his belt. Paying in advance— something was wrong here. The sky had barely turned blue, but he watched the dock more warily than ever before.

Out of the corner of his eye he saw two urchins, too young for their sex to be clear, giggling and pressing near the boat. Probably daring each other to touch it. But even urchins could be trouble. He walked over, staff in hand. One child wriggled back at the sight. The other stared, mouth agape. When the staff tapped the dock, he bolted.

Man won't complain about not getting his money's worth, thought Kyre, sitting again. He leaned the staff against the side. And there was no way quicker to draw thieves than to appear asleep.

Or even to sleep. He rose to pace along the boat. Keeping watch was weary enough business that he had to keep awake. He considered vendors as the hours rolled by and the sun rose, but he could not haggle much, not when he could not leave the boat.

He bought some water midmorning, from a vendor who smiled impishly at realizing she had him captive.

Men came by the boat soon after, and stood about, talking. Their clothing was not fine, but better than a dockhand's. Kyre watched them with narrowed eyes. After a third sidelong glance he stalked over and summoned his memories of how the boat owners talked. "My lords, the owner of the boat has left, and I do not know when he will return." His voice rang out and turned more than one head. "Leave me a message, and I will get it to him. After all, my lords, I would not like to keep great men such as yourself waiting like messenger boys."

A vendor snickered. Angry color in their faces, the men retreated. Kyre sat. The sun was still climbing, and having made his position clear, he was likely to have a long day. Many a man had hired a less watchful guard and not suffered for it.

He rose before an hour had past, and continued to walk. He could wear himself out that way—he would need even more water, as well—but if he grew stiff, he would have no chance should an attempt be made on the boat in earnest.

And there was nothing like an alert guard to prevent an attack before it happened.

Kyre grinned, turned, and saw something out of the corner of his eye: a shimmer. Like and unlike a mirage—the sunlight was wrong for one—and Kyre knew of thieves with enough coins to buy invisibility spells. He laid on to the thin air, and his staff hit a solid body with a thud. It yielded like flesh, and a grunt came out of the air before him.

Something cracked on his head from behind. The staff fell from his fingers as he collapsed to the deck, too dazed to rise.

"Knave," muttered the thin air.

"Going to blame him for your folly? You knew he was a guard. Give me a hand."

"This damned turtle had better be worth it."

The second speaker snorted. "Wait till we get to the island before you maunder. Now, we have to act."

Invisible hands took him up—he smelled the men he could not see—and dropped him to the dock. His staff clattered beside him. His stomach wrenched. About, he heard exclamations from the vendors, and the boat cast off, the ropes undone by invisible hands. Someone bolted, shrieking about ghosts and monsters, and Kyre heard others hurry off more quietly. Wincing, he pushed up off the dock. The boat had already set sail, though he could still see no one on board. About Kyre, those who had not fled gawked.

Wincing from bruises, Kyre rose to his feet. He had never seen such a thing before. And then it struck him: they had stolen the boat. The boat he had been hired to guard.

Kyre did not move. That had never happened to him before, either. If it had, he would not have been hired for this, because he would have starved. No one would hire a failure.

His hand went to his belt. No one stole from him, either the boat he guarded or his good name. He would follow and retrieve the boat, and win back his reputation. His fingers picked out the silver bit. Though his good pay would not be so good. He would spend most of the money renting a new boat.

How long can you live on one silver bit? came a sardonic thought.

When Kyre sailed up to the dock, set to follow the thieves, the vendors shouted from their stalls. Even a couple of the richer merchants emerged from their stores' shade. One—Benya, Kyre recalled—raced out to grab his arm. "He was here. The man whose boat it was. We told him." Her eyes were large. "He cursed *himself*. Said they were too much for you, and he shouldn't have left you where you had to face them."

And after I asked if the boat had anything I should know about. Kyre grimaced. Benya looked impressed now, but that would not help him when all they remembered was his failure.

She shook her head. "He was a wizard—had wizard things on that boat. And *he* said it would be hard to follow the thieves."

"But he could?"

"Wizard," said Benya. "And he said it was the island, and he could get there today."

Only one island within a day's journey, thought Kyre.

The rented boat sailed over the beige and yellow sands, if a little slowly in the low wind. Kyre surveyed the horizon. A wizard might find the thieves easier than a boy of the docks could, but the boy, who knew where the island was, might find it more easily than a man who didn't know. Kyre snorted. He hired me, he thought. He should have waited for me.

The sun loomed, orange and enormous, in the west. A ship stood black against it, and Kyre turned his boat to avoid her path, but not too far. A low island stood against the sky, too.

"Ahoy the boat!" A sailor waved to him as he slid by.

Kyre's eyebrows went up. He waved back.

The sailor gestured at the island. "'Ware the island. Magic's afoot!"

They revealed themselves, thought Kyre, feeling stunned. Whatever they did, they were not afraid to show that magic was being worked here.

He waved back, and the sailor went off, seeming content that he had done good for his fellow man. Kyre grinned. So he had. Even if his intention had been warn him off, not to tell him where he needed to go. Kyre looked up at the sail and whistled. There might be nothing in the tale that it could summon a wind, but there might be, and he could use haste in getting to the island.

And once he had recovered the boat from thieving wizards, everyone on the docks would want to hire him.

The island was low, with gaps of orange-red sand here and there in a shore of orange-red rock. The setting sun cast enormous shadows. Kyre crouched in the boat as he picked out one space as sand, not the fine stuff of the sea but a shoreline, a place that would not swallow him. He beached the boat there. It took care to find where the sand would let him stand, but Curgan would listen to no pleas about his boat being damaged, and the stone looked jagged. He pulled the boat further up on the beach, listening.

No sound came over the wind. If he were too coward to leave the boat, he should never have wasted good coin on hiring it. He went to hunt.

He crouched low among the stones. The island had enough gullies and ravines that he could sneak about, and a handful of bushes or two, though short on leaves, handed him more places to hide. It did not take long to find the stolen boat. The thieves had drawn it up on a larger beach. Once he got to the right ravine, the thieves' voices echoed against the stone, disputing how to break the spell on the chest. The breeze came from them and smelled of heated metal.

Kyre edged closer. He had to see them to plan.

A hand slapped over his mouth, and a strong arm went about his waist. Kyre started to struggle, but his assailant got him off his feet, and with no leverage, almost before he knew what had happened. He still struggled, out of pride, as he was dragged into the shelter of the rocks.

"Be still," the man who had hired him said.

Kyre stopped fighting. The man released him, and Kyre looked at him with wary eyes. He acted as if he knew the thieves. He had to know them better than Kyre did

"Leave." His voice was low but intense. "You should not have come. These wizards are beyond you."

What did this man know of the docks? Thinking that hiring Kyre meant that Kyre could let him be robbed and do nothing?

"No one robs me," said Kyre, drawing his knife. The man looked taken aback. "Don't you know how much my name means to me? Did you think I'd let these knaves drop it in the dust? I took your coin."

The man's tongue touched his lips. After a moment, he said, "You'll not stop them with only that knife."

Kyre shrugged. He could not let this man know that he had never killed before. "I'll help you."

"I know what I'm doing."

Kyre's lip curled. "Like you knew when you left me to guard? Without even a warning? Didn't know there'd be magic till I saw them shimmer. If I didn't know the spell, I'd never have guessed. I'd have let them steal the boat without a blow."

The man looked strangely at him, and then at the knife.

"Learned to use it from a soldier," said Kyre. "He always said, it was amazing how little it took to kill a man." He met the man's gaze. Old Anzar had also said, it was amazing how much it took to kill a man, but he would not repeat that here.

The man looked at the sky. The sun had turned almost scarlet. "Go home. If you wish to serve me, you can bear back news of my doings. My—house might be glad to hear—"

"Don't know your name," said Kyre.

After a long minute, the man said, "My name is Trist of Blaike."

"Your house going to pay enough for me to live on? Forever?" When Trist flinched, Kyre said, "Starving will kill me just as dead."

Trist's face worked, and he turned to Kyre as if he had made a decision. "They wish to cast death magic. The—thing in the box will help them." He met Kyre's gaze. "They will get into the box, but then I will be able to use the contents as well—provided they do not stop me."

"Let 'em try to stop you. I'll knife them," said Kyre. He stifled his qualms. He had never needed to kill before, but when he need to fight, he had. When the man said nothing, Kyre said, "You going to say that's—" He remembered how wizards talked. "*Not wise.*"

Slowly, Trist shook his head.

A good way to deal with wizards, then, Kyre thought. I'll remember it, next time a wizard tries to steal from me. Then—

"What happens when a spell stops?"

Trist ran a hand through his hair. "You shouldn't come; you should go home. It's ugly when a spell stops. Worst for the spell-caster, but it's hard on anyone—"

"Harder than starving?" His hand tightened on his knife.

Trist studied him. Then he said, "Follow me." He walked on without glancing back to see if Kyre obeyed. He kept to the ravines, as if he feared being seen—and then a light, like a fire, flared ahead. Trist let his breath out, slowly.

Kyre studied it. Then a breeze came toward them. It stank like a graveyard, and Kyre gagged.

"Go home," said Trist. "It will only get worse."

Kyre shook his head. Trist did not look surprised.

Kyre and Trist sat in the ravine, as far back as they could and still see the beach. The two wizard thieves emerged from the boat, into the firelight. With some awkwardness, they carried a large turtle, carved of stone. Firelight gleamed on its smooth surface and made its color impossible to tell. They laid it down by the blaze.

They started to chant.

After a moment Trist said, in grim confirmation, "A death spell." He started to chant as well. Kyre left him and slid closer to the fire. Spells might range far, but throwing his knife was a good way to lose it. He held the blade low, where it would not catch the firelight, and recalled everything that Anzar had told him of knife fights, and every time he had had to use it. The night breeze smelled of smoke, and another, charnel stench. His hand tightened on the hilt. He wasn't going to show himself where those wizards could see him.

The chant broke in half suddenly, one voice going silent. One thief rose. "Somebody's interfering." His voice was low with menace, and he surveyed the rocks.

The other thief, still chanting, nodded. The first one started into the stones, as if into the alleys of the city. Kyre looked about. Nothing handy for an ambush, and no telling what spells that man could cast if given a moment.

Kyre looked back where he had come. On the other hand, if something distracted him. . . . Kyre crept back toward Trist, keeping to the shadows.

The thief followed but did not seem to spot him. He stopped and looked about, and then, as Kyre heard Trist's chant, the thief leapt forward, toward the sound. Kyre pulled back, with care to be quiet. The thief did not glance aside as he rushed toward

Trist. Even when Kyre's foot scrapped on stone, he did not turn. Kyre lunged and clamped a hand over his mouth, to keep him from spells. The man thrashed against him, Kyre did not think he could hold him a minute longer, and then the man muttered words against his hand. Kyre pulled the knife up and into his throat. The flesh gave, and the knife drove deeper. Whatever the man tried to shout, it drowned in a gurgle, and blood splattered over Kyre's hand. And then, as suddenly as a match lighting, the knife seared his hand. His fingers jerked away before he could think; then, feeling colder than a winter night, remembering Anzar's tales of men trapped under corpses, Kyre jumped back. The body fell.

Kyre stood a minute. He had never killed anyone by that trick before. His heart beat faster than it had when he struck the blow. He had never killed anyone before.

He had remembered every trick Anzar had taught him. He dragged in a deep breath. The graveyard smell was bad, again, but he could not take his eyes from the body. He had seen men stabbed before, and even with the blade in the wound, the body did not bleed much. Kyre swallowed and crouched to retrieve the knife. It felt cool again, but the sand under it—even by the fire's stray light, it looked scorched. His hand reached for it, hesitated, and touched. He jerked it away. He felt glass.

Trist had warned him that breaking spells could be bad.

And the graveyard smell grew worse.

He yanked out the blade. The blood on it already looked dried, but he looked about. Death spell, he thought. Somebody was going to die, any way it fell out—maybe several somebodies. And chanting rose behind him. The surviving thief chanted as loudly as both of them had, or louder. The stones hid everything but the firelight, striking the higher rocks.

Kyre's back prickled. That didn't mean the thief hadn't seen him kill the other. The man was a wizard—no telling what he could see. Kyre crouched and hurried to Trist. The firelight

showed how pale his face was. He chanted and did not stop even
to look at Kyre.

Only a damn fool gets himself between two wizards, Kyre
thought. He'd tell the brats at the docks that, when he got back.
He looked down at the bloodied knife. Too late now. If he tried
to run, the wizard-thief would see him sail, and the wind
wouldn't move him fast enough to get away from the spell. He
doubted any wind could move fast enough.

If he attacked, the wizard would see him coming. The fire sat
in the middle of the sand. But Trist's spell might strike while the
wizard was casting his—on him.

Trist's spell might not strike in time to save him.

Got any better ideas? Kyre asked himself. He walked back
through the rocks. They were high; he had no need to crouch.

At the beach, Kyre stopped in the rocks' shadow to look once
more. The charnel smell hung heavy on the air. The wizard thief
had risen to his feet and chanted on. He looked toward the
rocks.

No surprise there, Kyre thought. I'll have to be quick. He
looked down. The sand was packed. The other thief had moved
quickly.

A loud crack came from the fire, and logs settled into place.
Distraction, thought Kyre, and leapt across the sand. A knife in
his throat would still his spell-casting.

The thief glanced at him. Kyre ran faster, his feet thudding
on the sand. The thief's voice rose louder, and his hands went
up. Kyre ran faster—he had never run so fast, not even fleeing
bullies three times his size. His hand tightened on the knife. The
thief's hands moved. For a moment, his words faltered, but Kyre
only watched his hands. They did not shield his throat.

Kyre struck from the side. They collided, and Kyre drove the
blade into his throat. It resisted harder than he would have
dreamed, his breath felt knocked out of him from the collision,
but his hand moved, driving the blade deeper.

It felt like a dark cloud swooped by him.

The thief made choked noises but did not fall. He pushed at Kyre.

He did not bleed, not even as much as the other one in the first moments. The blade was still in the wound. Kyre pulled at the knife. It had driven deep and did not yield easily, but the wizard's hands moved, and Kyre did not want to find he could cast spells by gesture. He yanked the blade out.

A gush of blood sent the wizard to his knees, and then to the sands.

Kyre drew a deep breath. The knife did not burn him, though he held it tightly. The other one must have done some kind of spell with heat, worse to break than this one's; that must have made the knife so hot, then. He looked down, at the blood that had splattered him. He shivered and thought of Trist. Best proof that he had, that he didn't let stuff be stolen, or he might end up having killed two men and still starving. He hurried through the stone, still crouching now and again, as if the fire could strike him down.

He almost stumbled over him. Trist lay silent, slumped on the rocks. Kyre touched his hand. It felt clammy.

He swallowed. The second thief had faltered in his spell before the knife had stopped it finally. Maybe—maybe Trist had broken the spell, and it had come after him.

Kyre shoved his knife back into the sheath. Not good, having the man who hired you die, even when you weren't a bodyguard. He rose. The boat had blankets. He could get those before he got the turtle back in the boat, or tied his hired boat to the stolen one.

The dawn was charcoal gray as Kyre set sail. Curgan's boat trailed behind the stolen one, and Trist, wrapped in blankets, lay on the deck with the turtle beside him. The breeze felt cold, but Kyre only moved the quicker to set the sail. When the boat sailed over the sands again, he sat in the prow and cleaned the knife. He felt colder than he had in the breeze. Had to kill them, he told himself. They would have killed Trist and me both. Had to kill them.

The litany did not warm him.

The light grew. When the island was only a line on the horizon, and they sailed over beige sand, Kyre looked at Trist. Pale. Paler than he had been, stopping the spell.

He stirred and looked at Kyre. "Paper. In that chest."

Kyre pulled out the paper, and the pen beside it—no inkwell. He laid them down.

Trist looked at his face and smiled. "Magic." He started to write. Ink flowed from the pen. "For you. For your services, and for arranging for my burial. . . ." He looked sharply at Kyre.

Kyre nodded. He could have Trist taken as a pauper, if worst came to worst; the priests buried enough of the port's dead as a good deed.

As if he had read Kyre's thoughts, the man smiled. "Coins in the chest. Enough to pay. After that—I bequeath to you the rest of what the boat holds, and the boat."

Kyre stared at him.

The man sank back. "The chest...." He gestured at the magical one. "Once I die, it will open only for you." He closed his eyes. "And the turtle—the turtle will make you rich beyond your *dreams.*"

He said nothing more. He still breathed, but he seemed asleep. Kyre went back to the sails. He might get him help on land; if he did that, Trist might survive and leave him nothing. If he dallied. . . .

Kyre tried to win more speed from the wind.

With the slight wind, the boat did not move quickly. Land had not come back into sight when noon came, and Trist died without speaking again.

Kyre warily took up the paper and tried the chest. It opened, and he put the paper within. He considered the turtle a minute longer.

He had a boat. Magic or not, he was rich beyond his dreams. The *pen* was more than he dreamed of.

And who needed thieves?

After a minute, Kyre put his hands on either side of the turtle. The polished stone felt slick. He took it with care to the side of the boat. Sand slid by him. He lowered it. For a moment, the stone sat on the sand like a turtle swimming.

Wouldn't last long, Kyre thought.

And it did not.

The turtle lifted its head as if sniffing the breeze. Its flippers moved against the sand. Swimming, Kyre realized blankly. Then it blinked its stony eyes and dove into the sands with a toss of its flippers. It left a ripple for a moment, and then the sands sealed up after it.

Kyre stared after it. It took a long time before he realized his mouth hung open.

Wonder if any of the wizards knew *that*, he thought.

Neither/Nor

Three of the upstairs rooms had lights on, but the porch light was dark. Marguerite Goldsmith glared at it; she had told her nieces when she was arriving for a reason. Muttering fiercely, she dropped her heavy suitcase on the porch and fumbled for the key. The lock was all but invisible against the dark wood of the door; Marguerite did not even try looking for it, but felt for it.

The door screeched open. There was no sound from upstairs. Marguerite picked up her suitcase and shifted it inside before reaching for the light. Pale yellow light filled the main hall, even though half the light bulbs had burned out and had not been replaced.

Marguerite had known that her nieces were disasters at housekeeping. She hadn't known it was *this* bad. Paths of dirt marked the way through discarded papers and coats tossed aside; shoes thrown by the stairs; houseplants wilting on the hall table.

Taking one look about, she shouted, "Lydia! Laura! Linnet!"

Two sets of footsteps clattered in the rooms overhead. Linnet came bounding down the stairs, her blond hair bouncing in twin braids down her back. "Aunt Tweet! You're here!"

Marguerite sniffed. "Well, of course I'm here. It's not every day that one is suddenly bequeathed with the guardianship of three nieces—or perhaps three pigs."

Lydia started down the stairs; she was very pale, especially next to Linnet's rosy cheeks. "We did our best," she said, and gestured hopelessly. "But with schoolwork and Daddy's illness and all. . . things just slid."

"And then there was the poltergeist," declared Linnet, quite proud of the long word.

Marguerite whipped her head around to look at her niece. "What?"

Linnet started hopping on one foot. "We went to sleep one night, just after Daddy went to the hospital, and in the morning, everything downstairs was a wreck, and the doctor that Child Welfare called in said it was a poltergeist—probably Laura. But they called in another doctor and he said it was just one of us making mischief." She grinned. "And they're both trying to prove who's right."

Since one has to be, Tweet thought, and smiled to herself.

"And things have gotten worse—sometimes dishes get broken and food gets spilled all over the place. So we've got *scientists* right here. Isn't it neat?"

Tweet suppressed her smile. "No, it isn't neat. In fact it's a pigsty. Go get Laura, Lydia; I don't care if you ruin her latest picture beyond hope of repair—go get her. I'm not staying in a mess like this."

Aunt Tweet swept into the kitchen as Lydia went off to fetch Laura. "Linnet!" The girl jumped before scurrying into the kitchen. Tweet pointed at the sink and the mounds of dirty dishes in it. "When was the last time someone did the dishes around here?"

"Err...I think Lydia did some last Sunday."

Aunt Tweet snorted. "Where are the towels, dear? You get to dry. I am going to have to empty out the sink before I wash anything."

The woman was up to her elbows in suds before Laura (still the same dreamy-eyed girl with pale brown hair, Tweet noted) and Lydia appeared, but without turning, Aunt Tweet set them to emptying the hall so they could mop it. "And water those plants as well!" she ordered as things started to move in the hallway. One of them hurried upstairs to fetch the water, and Tweet turned her attention back to the dishes.

"It's certainly going to impress the scientists," Lydia observed. "One of them was complaining to Child Welfare. . . ."

"The scientists?" Aunt Tweet asked sharply, turning. Laura hesitated in the middle of hanging up a coat.

"Why, yes, they're coming tonight," observed Laura. She titled her head to one side. "I had forgotten."

Tweet snorted. "Well, you can turn on the porch light for them, even if you couldn't for me."

Half an hour later, the hall was half-way respectable. Tweet put a hand through her hair. "I've still got to make up my bed," she muttered. She cast a glance at her nieces. "And we've still got to do the rest of the house."

The doorbell rang. "I'll get it," Lydia said. Laura hesitated with her hands full of books. Linnet turned from putting the last glass in the cabinet. She sat perched on the counter, the towel hanging in her hand, as the two men came in. Aunt Tweet folded her arms and contemplated the men.

"Dr. Pettifogger, Dr. Gobbledygook, good evening. Our aunt is here now."

"I see, I see—this sudden burst of housecleaning is her handiwork?" said a man's voice, jovially.

"My sister's rolling over in her grave from the mess," announced Aunt Tweet, turning a little but keeping her hands in the sudsy water. "And you two are?"

A tall thin man in a business suit sniffed. "I am Dr. Horatio Pettifogger; I am here to investigate Dr. Gobbledygook's claims with regard to your nieces."

Dr. Gobbledygook shrugged and spread out his hands. "Your nieces have told you of the unusual occurrences in this household?"

"Nothing unusual about trouble-making," Pettifogger muttered.

"When Child Welfare investigated after your brother-in-law went into the hospital, it seemed clear that one of your nieces is manifesting poltergeistic abilities." He looked at his notebook. "Probably Laura. I have been attempting to confirm the paranormal aspect."

Pettifogger broken in. "Nothing paranormal about adolescent mischief. I am quite certain that Lydia is causing the commotion by perfectly normal means. And it would be Lydia—the most apparently calm child clearly has the most repressed emotion."

Lydia did not repress her glare at the doctor's back.

"Uh, Aunt Tweet, the mop and stuff are in the cellar," said Laura, interrupting.

"So get them, dear," said Tweet, and turning back to the doctors, dismissed them. "I have to get this house into decent shape." She smiled vaguely and went back to remembering where the sheets were kept—if the girls had remembered to do enough laundry.

Pettifogger, fretting with his briefcase, cleared his throat. "We are figuring out which it is."

"If either." Her voice was dismissive.

Gobbledygook frowned. "It has to be one."

Tweet smiled. "That's hardly an exhaustive list of causes," she observed. *Although*, she thought, *I don't think you'll believe my explanation.*

Pettifogger reddened and puffed up. "Well, Ms. Goldsmith, no one's suggesting anything else."

Tweet spread her dripping hands. "Then, by all means, attempt to identify it."

Linnet sat in the porch swing, her feet reaching just far enough to push it herself. She did not remember to push often; her attention was concentrated on the papers in her lap.

". . .there were no more incidents of poltergeist activity," she read from Gobbledygook's report. Marguerite, sitting on the porch steps in the last sunlight of evening, barely listened, concentrating on the hem she was mending. "Clearly the arrival of Miss Goldsmith and its promised renewal of ordinary routines relieved the subconscious stress causing the phenomenon." She shrugged and picked up her lemonade.

A minute later, she lifted her face from the glass. "Did Dr. Pettifogger send you a report, too?"

"Yes," said Aunt Tweet, not looking up from her sewing. "Said Lydia couldn't cause any more trouble with me sleeping in the master bedroom." She snorted. "Means the same thing— they can't recognize the real cause when they see one."

"But they didn't see one." Linnet gulped her lemonade. "At least I didn't see one."

"Well, they're scientists; they're supposed to deduce these things from evidence." Aunt Tweet laid aside the sewing to get a saucer from the cabinet and milk from the fridge. Linnet watched her intently as she set the saucer by the fireplace.

"We haven't got a cat," Linnet announced.

"I know, Linnet. To bed."

Linnet scampered off to bed.

The grandfather clock woke Linnet at midnight. She lay in bed a minute longer before she tried creeping out into the hallway. She slept the end of the hallway farthest from the stairway, but Laura, Lydia, and Aunt Tweet slept still—Aunt Tweet snored. Carefully, Linnet walked down the hallway and halfway down the stairs.

The little light Aunt Tweet left on in the kitchen was still on, and clearly showed the quite contented brownie lapping up the milk.

One Name

"We have to do *something* with Sophie's baby," complained Angelica.

Sophie, sitting the back of the solar with her baby sleeping in its cradle, did not look up from the letters she was penning for her father-in-law. That had been Angelica's plaint ever since the baby had been born.

Besides, Angelica was right. Sophie had no more idea than her mother-in-law what to do with a baby for which they were too poor to hire a nurse. She and Gabriel had wed to secure the line when everyone had thought Gabriel's elder brother Michael had died; but now Michael was back, and Michael's wife had produced twins, Gabriel had died, and Gabriel's wife had produced a baby girl they could not provide for.

"Why not send them both to the convent? That was where Sophie was going to go anyway," offered Vera, Michael's wife, in an infinitely practical voice.

"Sophie can," said Angelica. "Her dowry is her own. But how do we produce one for the baby? When we are so badly off we can't persuade anyone to be the baby's godmother!"

And that was it, in the nutshell. Sophie's fingers tightened on the pen. This was the point at which, in every fairy tale, some mysterious man arrived and offered to stand as godfather.

The baby wailed. Sophie scrambled to her feet and across the room to pick her up, and the baby began to calm. Sophie looked out at the barren snowscape.

Sleigh bells jingled in the courtyard, startling Sophie; surely no one traveled in this weather to the poorest noble house in the land!

A red sledge, drawing by two golden horses, glided into the courtyard and stopped, one horse's tossing head framed in the window beside Sophie. For a second she thought it had red eyes; then the grooms hustled up to take them, and Sophie realized that she must have been mistaken; Ed would have thrown a fit at an enchanted horse, even if none of the other grooms had noticed. Still, Sophie moved closer: there was something on the sledge, and it was no coat-of-arms—nor a merchant's mark, either!

The grooms moved so that Sophie got little more than a glimpse of the golden rune. She bit her lip. It did look like a wizard's rune.

"So much for my *useless* studies," she muttered.

"Sophie, what is it?" Angelica asked, her voice high and breathless.

Sophie turned to her mother-in-law. "A visitor."

"Faery gold, as it is called, has not set aside its moral nature with its mortal seeming. All metals and other things are corruptible; gold is immortal. For this reason, that which transforms base metal into gold truly will also turn moral men immortal. Howbeit, the faery gold is transformed by a lesser transformation, the which is not permanent. Where other things so transformed rot after their new seeming, gold can but revert. . . ."

"Lady Sophie!"

Sophie jerked her head up from the book, startled by Jennet's voice. The elderly maid bobbed a curtsey and said, "His Grace will be seeing you in his office."

The lady quickly put the book aside. Sir Marcel Silvermarsh wrote better than any man of the Northlands, where their guest's sledge came from, but he did so at great length.

"And you, silly woman," she told herself, "were side-tracked from your quest to name our quest by her run—by the faintest of sidetracks. Like that chapter on the chapel of St. Jewel."

Lucius was very jovial when Sophie arrived. "Ah, good, you are here, daughter. This woman, Mariah, she's a merchant of great prosperity—has offered to be the baby's godmother. Not only that—she has need of an heir, so she'll raise the baby herself."

"Has need of an heir?" Sophie heard her voice say. This woman a merchant? No caravan, no guards, no goods—what was Mariah supposed to be trading in?

Mariah nodded. "I have a certain prosperity," she said, her voice low and rich. "I have, also, need of an heir as the news I have here has told me." She lifted a piece of parchment from her lap. "It says that my kinsfolk have *selected* an heir for me. I have no wish to give anything to that fool. I will gladly foster my goddaughter and make her my heir."

What wizard needs an heir? But Sophie said nothing. Mariah looked her up and down. Sophie stood there, a pale woman, whom black did not become, her lambent gold hair drawn into a severe bun. The wizard smiled: Sophie would go into the convent with no trouble at all.

"Me mum said she looks just like a fairy-tale witch," said Jane breathlessly, as she brushed out Sophie's hair.

Sophie, barely listening to the maid, said, "She is." Then she gasped as Jane pulled on a tangle.

"She does look like one? You think so? Mum said you thought fairy tales were silly. . . ."

"No," said Sophie, absently, as her thought went back to her problem. "I meant she is a wizard. She has magical runes on her sledge."

The hairbrush clattered on the floor. "Why, you can't believe that, me lady! Even Mum knows that they're fairy tales!"

Sophie smiled. "Your mum has utmost respect for my book-learning. I assure you, I saw the runes."

Jane's eyes grew enormous. "But what's she gonna do to baby Mariah? No wizard needs no heir!"

Sophie grabbed Jane's hand. "Listen." The maid nodded. "Mariah has a paper; she said it had the reason why she needed an heir. She lied about what it said, but it might hold the truth."

Jane nodded, her eyes still wide.

"She knows I'm one of the family, but all she will see of you is that you're a maid. If you could go to her room. . . ."

"And steal from a wizard? I wouldn't dare!" The maid stepped back, her hands going to her pale face.

"Think, Jane!" Sophie exclaimed, grabbing Jane's hand. "She's going to take little Mariah. Don't you want to keep the baby safe from the wizard?"

Sophie took the nearest chair to the library's fire to read the letter. Mariah may have assumed she was illiterate, but the wizard would guess where her letter went. After a quick glance over her shoulder, Sophie unrolled it to see vivid writing, in ink of black, gold, blue red.

To Her Wisdom, the Wizard of the North Winds, from the Reader of Runes:

In response to your query, I must inform you that your name has again appeared in the Book of the Angel of Death, that you will die this coming year on the Feast of Candlemas in the third hour of the morning. I advise haste in the necessary preparations.

Sophie stared for a minute, hoping that the letter would abruptly begin to make sense. How far could this wizard raise the baby if she died within three months? and how could the wizard's name appear *again*, if, when it first appeared, she should hae died.

Her lips moved as she reread the letter. The Book of the Angel of Death—it almost rang a bell. Briskly, Sophie rolled up the letter. She did not have much time to puzzle it out. Mages were unpredictable but powerful. The best chance would be to look through the books that Gabriel had carefully kept from his father's attention—the books on wizardry, by the wizards. They might not confess all, but they would confess much.

And she doubted that Mariah intended to leave an heir.

The baby squalled again. Sophie stuck the letter into her volume as a bookmark and hurried over. Angelica would throw a fit if she thought Sophie neglected the baby, even in favor of finishing her husband's last work, and might even ban her from the library.

"Which would really be neglecting you, munchkin."

The baby gurgled.

"I've never seen a baby like attention as much as you." Sophie put the baby on her hip and returned to the book she had been reading: *The Book of Jacobionous.*

"Of such impudence are the mages that they presume to read the Book of the Angel of Death, therein learning the hours of their own deaths, and earning the righteous enmity of Almighty God, who had forbidden such presumptuous pryings into His benevolent plans."

Sophie faithfully read on. Jacobionous rambled on for many pages about the evils the mages were able to do with the powers of their conjured demons, but did not return to the Book of the Angel of Death.

Sophie sighed. At least she knew that Mariah was indeed about to die—again.

"How could anyone trick the Angel of Death?" she asked.

The baby answered very intelligently. Sophie kissed it and put it back in the cradle. There were very few books on sorcery left. Idly, Sophie picked up a book on the Northlands and flipped through it; falling open on a chapter on superstitions, it caught her eye with the assertion that trolls fear milk, and she began to slowly turn the pages.

"It is held among the North Lands, that a babe may not be named after one still living, for the Angel of Death might confuse the twain when it comes for the elder, and take the babe when the elder must die."

Sophie remembered to breathe a minute later.

Sophie licked her lips as she reached for the door latch to His Grace's office. True, Lucius did not think much of her learning—it had been Gabriel who encouraged her—but he would have to listen to this.

He would have to.

Then she heard the wizard within the office. "Your daughter-in-law spends much time in the library," said Mariah, coolly.

"Too much," said Lucius, heartily. "I told Gabriel not to encourage her. . . well, we'll ship her off to the convent soon enough. It's a good thing you'll have the baby; I'm not sure Sophie could be trusted as a mother. Too many odd notions. Why, she really believes that there's magicians!"

Sohpie's hand fell from the latch. She would only be telling Mariah that she knew what the wizard was up to. Lucius had settled his little problem.

Her lips tightened. She should have known better in the first place; she began to walk briskly away, planning. She could take little Mariah and run—but Lucius would no doubt think her mad and hunt her down; and even after the baby was baptized, it might not stop the wizard's plans. On the other hand, the wizard lived in the North; surely, she could gather up enough money to follow, especially if she claimed to be a pilgrim. It would not matter that she went slower; Mariah had months to go before she sacrificed the baby to her own prolonged life.

Unless Mariah lived somewhere out of human lands. Sophie's step faltered. A wizard who could trick the Angel of Death must have powers. Sophie's imagination conjured up a tower of ice on the highest mountain in the world, with the North Wind blowing about it.

"Are you certain of this woman's plans?" demanded the priest again.

"Certain," said Sophie. Her knees ached; she had been kneeling in the confessional booth too long. But she needed someone to talk to, and even if the priest decided that she was mad, it was under the seal of the confessional.

"Certainly it is written that He will protect you and your daughter from the works of the Evil One." The priest sounded shocked. Sophie did not doubt it; how often had someone come to him with a tale of this sort of sorcery?

"It is further written, You shall not put the Lord your God to the test," Sophie said, sharply. Her vague ideas were becoming solid.

"What can you do against this evil woman?" the priest protested. "The Lord will yet deliver this babe."

The Lord might deliver every babe in trouble, Sophie thought, but generally into the hands of the Angel of Death. She did not say it. Her thoughts were finally clear. She received the priest's final instructions and went to say her penance.

"I baptize you Mariah in the name of the Father and the Son and the Holy Ghost."

The new Mariah bawled with vigor in Sophie's arms. The older Mariah smiled pleasantly, but coolly.

Sophie's lips drew into a fine line. Mariah had drawn the battle lines.

At the banquet after, she found it easier than she had expected to get to her feet and announce that she intended a pilgrimage prior to taking vows: to the shrine of St. Jewel.

"But that's so far to the north," Angelica exclaimed. "Why not some closer saint, like Saint Marie-Elise?"

Lucius laughed. "It's not so far; my lady Mariah lives farther from there."

"Why, they're going in the same direction. . . . "

Sophie interrupted, her tongue almost tripping over itself as she explained that she would be going on foot. Mariah smiled. Sophie glanced at the wizard, wondering if the woman knew why Sophie would not go with her: if she traveled with Mariah, the wizard would be able to leave her at the chapel.

Leave her, that is, if the wizard *knew* that Sophie was traveling with her.

The horses unquestionably had red eyes. Now that the stable boys were elsewhere, what spell Mariah had used had faded. Blood-red fires blazed in their eyes; Sophie almost expected to see sparks flying over the glossy golden hides. The horses arched their necks and snorted at her, but Sophie stepped quickly into the darkened stable. She had left on her pilgrimage that morning; if she had lingered on the threshold, she would have to explain why she lurked about the stable at an ungodly hour when she ought to have been miles away.

She hurried past the horses. The sledge sat in the back of the stable. Rich furs poured over the red velvet of the seat, but behind them, beneath the seat, there was enough room for a slender woman, if she curled herself up.

Sophie did. She had worn her warmest cloak for the pilgrimage; she would need every bit of it that night.

Resolutely, she closed her eyes; she would need to be rested in the morning. She began to drift off to sleep when it occurred to her that horses that strange might be able to talk to their mistress.

A drowsy Sophie looked carefully at the wizard where she stood in the courtyard, the baby in her arms. The wind stirred the longest strands of her black hair, but did not even twitch her heavy crimson robe.

Sophie returned to the prayer she had begun when she had decided that she would not try to get back to sleep. "I arise today through God's strength to pilot me," and you had best be strong indeed, God; "God's might to uphold me, God's wisdom to guide me. . . ."

Mariah swept toward the sledge and stepped aboard. Sophie drew in shallow breaths. The wizard sat, placed the baby beside her, pulled the furs over her lap, covering Sophie's vision, and shook the reins. The horses began to canter out of the courtyard.

Minutes later, they still glided along the road. Sophie let a long breath out; they must be out of sight of the castle by now, so no fear of being seen had kept the horses silent. She curled up even closer to the back of the sledge.

The sledge tilted as it began to rise. Sophie frowned, trying to remember a road that would have a hill this steep, this close to the castle. Then she realized that the horses' hooves were no longer making a sound against the road.

One of her hands froze against the sledge's floor. A little tendril of mist wove its way past Mariah's golden furs—except that it wasn't mist, but cloud.

Sophie swallowed, hard, and resumed the prayer. "God's shield to protect me, from the snares of the devil, from everyone who wishes me ill, near or afar, alone or in a multitude. . . ."

Hours later, the horses' hooves clattered again on stone. Sophie, with the very tips of her fingers, pushed the fur fractionally aside. Black stone walls, polished like mirrors, loomed overhead as the horses trotted down the courtyard into stables. Mariah tossed the fur aside (Sophie shrank back) and walked out of the stable with the baby Mariah. No stable boy emerged; the red leather straps began to undo themselves, and within a minute, the horses ate docilely in their stalls while the sledge slid into the back room, the door snicking quietly shut behind it.

Sophie stretched her legs out. It must have been longer than it seemed; they moved reluctantly. Sophie glanced back at the seat. Or perhaps the sledge was smaller than it seemed. Carefully, she stretched her arms and legs. The back room barely held the sledge and the red harness neatly hung on the wall. Her arms could brush against the black roof. It was cold, slick, and uncanny under her fingers, and a long minute before her hand felt normal again.

Mariah was in the castle proper. Briskly, Sophie headed for the door. "Christ be with me, Christ before me, Christ behind me. . . ."

The horses' eyes gleamed red. Their arrogant golden heads glowed, and as Sophie stood, her hand paralyzed on the back room's door, a golden flame licked up from one mane. Then she wondered how she could have missed it: the horses were forms of fire, with coals for eyes, and flames for man and tail.

She stepped into the stable, and one horse snorted and turned its head. Sophie froze, but it began to stamp and paw. As the horses began to whinny, Sophie scrambled for the exit Mariah had left by; once in the corridor, she took the first door.

Mariah swept past the room where Sophie hid, to declaim loudly that she'd let the horses know she would have no more of this; they were to be silent!

Sophie let out a long sigh of relief, but even then she remembered to sigh quietly, lest the imperious woman sweeping down the corridors hear her. Carefully, she walked to where she could see Mariah return from the stables, and saw the hallway's candles light themselves with icy white flames as the wizard walked back, and a sharp little breeze open the door before her.

The same breeze closed the door behind Mariah, but Sophie did not move for several long minutes, and when she did, she was glad that the candles did not light, though she skinned her knees on a side-table and nearly bumped her nose on the door.

"Hush, little baby, don't say a word," crooned Mariah's nursemaid, and little Mariah seemed almost willing to be hushed.

Solemnly, she watched the little figure carved from an apple tree root wave its twig arms over her.

Sophie stood silently in the empty corner of the room, watching. The nursemaid would not notice her; none of the beings that animated the castle noticed her. Perhaps they assumed that Mariah had conjured her; perhaps they could not be curious. She had crept about like a mouse the first days, until she realized they would take no more notice of her than of a mouse—the only cat in the castle was the wizard.

Hiding from Mariah took more effort; the wizard's castle had fewer rooms than the king's, or even Sophie's own family's, only seven or eight. The first day, Sophie had realized which was the important one: midnight blue marble held the golden patterns of two inscribed pentacles. Sophie walked softly about it, and the kitchen and the baby's room, waiting for the day.

Until she realized, a week or two later, that she had lost track of the days, and though she knew what the important day was, she could not know how far off it was.

She took to haunting the baby's room, then, curling up in the corner beside the wardrobe, leaving only to raid the kitchen, hoping that Mariah's enchantments would take long enough so that Sophie could return to save the baby. How, she did not know yet. Once or twice, she had slipped into the library and tried to read some of Mariah's books. But the wizard read on many subjects, and it would have taken a concerted search to find the right book—a search that Mariah could not have missed.

Tonight, at least, Sophie had been safe going to the kitchen; Mariah danced on the snow outside with green flickering spirits like the Northern Lights. Sophie twitched aside a curtain to watch the imperial woman, surrounded by a cascade of dancing emeralds, dancing with herself in total self-absorption.

Little Mariah slept. Sophie sat. She almost wanted to sleep herself, but the letter had said it would be in the wee hours of the morning. Dutifully, she stayed awake, watching the baby; it was easier now than it had been the first week.

An hour later, Mariah swept into the room. The nursemaid jumped to its feet, but the wizard snapped her fingers without looking at the conjuration, and a pile of broken wood fell to the ground. Eyes completely focused on only one target, the wizard swept up the baby and left the room. The nursemaid did not twitch.

Sophie, her heart pounding, got to her feet. She had been keeping watch only to keep practice; she had been certain that it could have been the month that she had waited.

On soft feet, she padded from the room, following Mariah into the conjuration room.

A cradle sat beside the larger pentacle. Mariah dumped the baby there and began to set up a fire in the pentacle. Little Mariah fully awoke and began to wail. Mariah poured some herbs into the wood.

Sophie stepped into the room carefully and began to walk around the pentacle. Would Mariah's total absorption let her steal the baby? And then they could be gone.

The wizard turned as Sophie reached the cradle. Sophie froze, but the other woman merely walked back to the other pentacle. Carefully, Sophie lifted little Mariah and scurried back into the corner.

The wizard reached out and tossed a handful of sparks into the larger pentacle. All missed the wood. Mariah's lips tightened; she tossed another handful, igniting the wood.

The fire licked the wood slowly. Mariah waited. Her eyes drifted over to the cradle. An eyebrow lifted.

It doesn't matter to her, Sophie realized in sudden terror. *It doesn't matter to her where the baby is!*

Mariah glanced over her shoulder at Sophie. "Leave the castle, if you think it will help." The wizard turned back to the fire, now blazing, and the pale gray smoke forming from it. Like sharp crystal, the words of an invocation fell from her mouth. The smoke hesitated in its climb, swirled, and reshaped. A person stood in the pentacle. Simple white robes swept the floor; pale golden hair gleamed, falling to its shoulder; sky-blue wings arched from its shoulder; and though it was neither male nor female, its face held an unearthly beauty. Sophie drew in a ragged, almost painful breath at its beauty.

It spoke, and its voice sound like the ringing of bells. "For what need have you summoned me here, Mariah, Lady of the North Winds?"

Mariah's voice grated by comparison. "Invisibility to angels, again."

"So soon?" It raised an eyebrow.

Sophie choked. It would not matter where the baby was; only where the wizard was. If the Angel of Death could not see the wizard, and sought a female named Mariah. . . .

"My Lord and my God, how can you permit this abomination?" Sophie muttered. The baby wailed again as Sophie hugged her tight, but the woman did not notice. The only thing that would help would be to stop the spell—but the devil would cast it, and she could not harm it, and she would surely die if she stepped within the devil's pentacle. Even guessing that she would have to be present to foil the wizard had done her no good!

"Lord Jesus Christ, have mercy on me." Sophie was barely aware that she had said the prayer.

Sonorous nonsense echoed from the devil's exquisite lips. Sophie glanced at Mariah's pentacle. The other one held the devil, or it could destroy both Sophie and the baby, so why did Mariah wait in a pentacle of her own?

The demon raised its hand. "On the woman Mariah, before me in this pentacle, let the power of invisibility to all angels and archangels and heavenly hosts be conferred."

Sophie took two steps forward. Her hand planted firmly in the middle of the wizard's back, she shoved the woman out of the pentacle.

The wizard whirled. Sophie, grim-faced, stood in the pentacle, her daughter in her arms.

"Let it be conferred, *now!*"

The devil disappeared. The baby did not. Sophie chucked her under the chin. "But I'm no angel, am I?"

Mariah's face contorted with fury. "You miserable wretch!" she screamed like some petty fishwife. Sophie stepped back as the wizard stepped forward.

The roof above was suddenly overshadowed by huge wings. After a confused impression of indigo and black, Sophie saw

Mariah crumpled to the floor before her, and an indigo feather drifting down to rest on little Mariah's blanket.

Were I You

Rosemary Whitney sat beneath the willow tree, her book in her lap; Annabelle, confident in her sister's obliviousness, skipped across the field with the breezes, her hands full of daisies.

"Don't step in the fairy ring," Rosemary called.

Annabelle stopped an inch from the mushrooms. "Oh, that's just an old superstition." She glanced back over her shoulder. Rosemary's book was open, but the woman was looking at her. How could Rosemary have looked up just then?

"So is walking under a ladder," Rosemary answered tartly, "and John still got a bucket of paint over his head."

Annabelle put her hands on her hips. "Anyway, we've got nothing to be afraid of. We're part fairy—as you know."

Rosemary said nothing. Her black hair was neatly put up, covering her ears, but they were still pointed—the legacy of an ancestral seduced maiden. Her mouth twitched. "Lady Jane did not find the fairies pleasant."

Annabelle came over by her sister to weave her daisy chain. "But the story's so *romantic*."

"I don't find the idea of wasting away from some rakehell romantic—and I dare say that Lady Jane found it even less romantic." Her finger marking her place, Rosemary swung her book in the air as she looked at her sister. "And nowadays—do you really find Mad Nan romantic, galloping up and down the highway when everyone else is trying to sleep?" Rosemary glanced down at the book to remember her place, then returned to her reading.

Annabelle did not argue the point. She frowned as she tied one of the daisies. "Is Mad Nan the daughter of Old Peg?"

"Old Peg?" Rosemary asked, preoccupied.

"The fairy woman that lived outside the nursery back at Green Ivy," Annabelle explained.

"I think she. . . ."

The church bells began to ring. Rosemary snapped the book shut. "We've been out far too long. I wonder Mother hasn't sent one of the servants after us." She rose to her feet. Annabelle jumped up in a shower of daisies, and the sisters hurried across the field to the road and down to the house. There was a gray horse to one side of it.

"Is that Mr. Newcastle's horse?" Annabelle asked curiously.

Rosemary felt the first touches of a blush to her cheek. "I think so."

"That's very odd," Annabelle declared. "He visited us two weeks ago, and he generally makes sure he visits all his parishioners in turn."

Rosemary slowed and turned her face away from Annabelle. Surely her face had to be scarlet. And Annabelle had to be able to guess why Henry Newcastle came so often.

Annabelle skipped on ahead, as oblivious to Rosemary's blushes as to any reason why the parson would come. Rosemary collected herself and followed. A thought came to her. She blushed again: perhaps Henry had come to speak with Father. . . .

Their father's voice came flying out the window. "I absolutely forbid you to tell her any of this nonsense!"

"What nonsense?" Annabelle asked, looking in the drawing room window.

Charles Whitney looked away from Henry to the window, quickly seeing Annabelle, but paid no attention to her. It was when he saw Rosemary join her that his florid face stiffened.

"Tell me what, Father?" she asked.

"Stuff and nonsense," Charles blustered. Henry shifted his weight; his face was pale but set.

"Father, I would rather hear what Mr. Newcastle has to say from him, than hear it from the maids." Her hand tightened on the book. "I am sure that everyone in the house has heard whatever it is."

"It is ill news," Henry said. He did not meet her eyes.

Rosemary felt her stomach freeze. She could not move for a second. If Annabelle had not been missing anything. . . if it had been her seeing too much. . . Rosemary swallowed and straightened. Then the only thing she could do was not make a fool of herself.

"I stayed with Mrs. Johnston last evening," Henry said, "and was coming home late. I saw Old Peg, holding her Unholy Court." He tried to meet her eyes, failed, and deliberately looked away. "She was half drunk. . . ."

Rosemary snorted; she did not care if it was unladylike. Old Peg was *always* drunk.

It almost brought a smile to Henry's face, but he went on "She boasted of her daughter, Mad Nan." He drew a deep breath. "Except that she said that Nan was not her daughter, that she had the first changeling that the fairies had gotten in centuries, that Mad Nan was the true Rosemary Whitney, traded for you on May Day."

Rosemary distantly supposed she must have turned pale— Annabelle had gasped in horror.

"It's nonsense, obvious nonsense," Charles blustered. "The woman is drunk half the time, and a scofflaw the rest! Was, even when Rosemary was a baby! Would lie under oath without qualm!"

"For God's sake, bring Miss Rosemary into the house and give her some brandy!" Henry said. Annabelle took her sister's hand and tugged; Rosemary felt herself suddenly able to move that much, at least. Once inside, her sister hovered over her while Charles fetched the brandy, and Henry stood in the background, miserable.

"old Peg is a dreadful old liar," Henry offered, finally. "All the fairy folk are."

Rosemary smiled at him a little and sipped the brandy. She supposed she would not have been able to bear it if he'd kept such a thing from her.

A circle of candlelight spilled around the table as Rosemary moved up the library's movable stairs to find the slim, hard-bound book. *The Natural History of Fairies* was tucked away in a corner, covered with dust-bunnies but easily found, since she had put it there herself after once reading it. No one else had been interested in the ramblings of an eccentric great granduncle on the fairy folk.

A draft ran across her ankles as she came down. She should have waited until morning. No matter that she had awakened in the middle of the night with the thought of this book obsessing her. The night was no time to read about the Good Folk.

The bland brown cover looked perfectly respectable. Half remembered paragraphs from its pages floated through her memory, but the only thing she was sure of was that it mentioned Old Peg. Her hands clenched it before she put it down on the library table. She could read it in the morning.

She reached for the candle and started out of the library. A line floated through her memory: "Old Peg something-or-other lied." Rosemary turned and stormed back to the table. She was going to get to the bottom of her memories.

At least it wasn't thundering, she thought. Smiling faintly, she began to scan the pages of ancient typeset and tales of milkmaids and four-leafed clovers.

". . . and the parson bound all those Fair Folk to never lie again, and among them were Jack of the Crossroads, Old Peg. . . ."

She felt very cold. He could have been mistaken in the tale, or it could have been a different Old Peg, but she looked at the lace on her nightgown, and the elegant furniture, and the fine library, with desperate eyes. Then she carefully put *The Natural History* and left the library.

"Father is taking it hard," observed Tom, leaning against a porch post.

Rosemary shrugged, her hand fretting the cloth of her skirt. Her brother had returned from the university that day, and been informed of Old Peg's story. "It is a serious matter."

"Serious indeed! Imagine wishing a sister like Mad Nan on me and Annabelle!"

Rosemary smiled wryly. "Well, she is, at any rate, not *my* sister." Tom straightened, indignant. "Nan would want her rights, though," she observed mildly.

"Rights?" His eyebrows went up. "Nothing's entailed; Father can leave it where he likes. And Nan certainly can't have Mr. Newcastle."

Rosemary turned scarlet. Tom smiled and started off, whistling. Rosemary watched him for a second, shaking her head more in amazement than in anger, before she returned her attention to her book.

The afternoon wound lazily on; the sun had begun to sink when Rosemary heard the hoof beats. They were distinctive enough; Mad Nan's horse could be recognized throughout the county. Rosemary clearly heard the horse pull up in front of the house. She did not turn, though, content with imagining Mad Nan dismounting, coming into the garden, coming up to the back porch.

"Good evening."

Rosemary started at the greeting. She turned.

Mad Nan grinned at her, her hands shoved into the pockets of her gypsy garb. Teeth flashed in a blood red mouth, in a face as pale as moonlight. Her black hair was pulled back into a braid, showing her pointed ears.

Though not much more pointed than Rosemary's own. Her hand resting on her amber skirt, Rosemary looked at the fairy and wondered if any of the resemblance was her frantic imagination.

Nan looked smug. "So. He told you."

"Certainly," Rosemary said. "I did not like it at first, but I had to know what tales Old Peg was telling."

"Tales, Miss Whitney?" Mad Nan laughed. "Tales?"

Rosemary said nothing. Old Peg would exchange a changeling for a child in a second.

"Your precious clergyman." Nan shook her head. "My precious clergyman, by rights. Mother told me all about it."

"You want to attend all the tea parties in the village? I would scarcely think that you would enjoy them," Rosemary answered, coolly. She felt a sudden pang; not so much for the tea parties as for all the ordered serenity of her life.

Nan's mouth twisted. "You have no right to be at them. You're not a Whitney." She tossed her head. "*I* do what I like."

"Keep everyone else from sleeping?"

"As if you humans were always so innocent of it," Nan retorted. "Your—*my* mother was fond of parties that disturbed Old Peg. Served her right when Old Peg changed us on Lammas."

Rosemary went white.

"You are sure of that?" Henry asked, his tea ignored on the table beside him.

"As sure that you heard Old Peg say May Day," Rosemary answered, and lifted her tea cup.

"Well, that settles the matter," declared Charles jovially. "Old Peg can't keep her tales straight. There's no way they can be true. Let Mad Nan press the matter as she likes."

Rosemary folded her hands in her lap. "True enough." But she could not forget the story in the *Natural History*.

Henry smiled. "I am sorry to have distressed you with the tale," he said, but his regret did not make it into his tone.

Rosemary nodded, but said, "Then I would not have known what to say to Nan." She got to her feet. Matter settled or no, she still felt jittery. Old Peg was garrulous and unscrupulous, yet Rosemary could remember no time that the fairy woman had been noted for lying.

She glanced out the window and realized a carriage had pulled up in front. "It's Sir Fitzwilliam," she said. Charles looked puzzled; the magistrate did not normally call on them.

A thin, white-haired man was welcomed in. "Mr. Whitney, I have come to you about a most distressing tale. One of those young Socialist—MacGregor—is spreading a fantastic tale about Miss Whitney."

Rosemary tilted her head and listened carefully.

"And about that drunkard fairy Old Peg. A story about a changeling."

Rosemary's eyebrows went up. "What day did Old Peg say she did it on?"

Sir Fitzwilliam blinked. "Miss Whitney. . . ."

Henry said, "We have heard the story before, and it *is* important."

Sir Fitzwilliam pondered it for a moment. "It was on Midsummer's Eve, but I don't see how that affects Miss Whitney's distressing position."

"She had claimed this twice before this month," Rosemary explained. "Once to Mr. Newcastle, and once to Mad Nan, but the days she gave did not match."

"Well, that doubtlessly puts an end to her claims," said Sir Fitzwilliam in satisfaction. There certainly was no need to have a drunken old woman testify against the daughter of one of the oldest families in the county."

Rosemary nodded graciously. "There is, however, reason to confront her, to make her tale clear."

Sir Fitzwilliam agreed. "Such libel should not be permitted. I will have the truth of her myself."

Rosemary's tongue ran over her lips. "I think. . . I think that would not be best. The woman is known to be a scofflaw; she would lie to you more readily than to another." She stopped and thought for a moment. Sir Fitzwilliam was certain not to think of Old Peg's speaking the truth. "I will speak to her myself."

The sunset was brilliant: crimson, scarlet, violet, gold, like the livery of a fairy court. Rosemary stood in the garden, feeling the dew wet her slippers. A suitable introduction to the matter, she thought; then scolded herself for dramatics. If she stepped in no fairy circle, she had nothing to fear.

"Rosemary?"

"Henry?"

The young clergyman came up and took her hand. "You are certain you must do this thing?"

Rosemary made an exasperated sound. "I would not decided on it otherwise. Let us go."

He pulled her hand up and kissed it.

Sit Fitzwilliam awaited them on the porch, with a servant to carry the lantern; she had not been able to argue out of having witnesses to her claim. Tom sat on the porch railing, whistling.

Rosemary nodded, and the expedition started down the lanes. Color faded from the sky; dusk gathered around them as they walked to Green Ivy.

The fairy gathering glowed in pale green light ahead of them. Rosemary stopped, laying a hand on Henry's arm. "Put out the light. I would just as soon they saw only me."

A minute later, she walked forward. Vines with luminescent flowers wound around ancient oaks, and fireflies danced over a company of hobs, pixies, and little folk, shaggy, misshapen, and uncanny. Cups of acorns were raised with fairy brews; fantastic banquets of mushrooms spread over a long table; frantic dancing to a faun's piping filled the clearing.

Rosemary remembered her legends and stopped outside the circle; the music was lively, but the dance could not trap her unless she stepped inside. She looked about. Even in this crowd, Old peg ought to be distinctive.

"Why, it's me darling daughter!" Rosemary turned to the shout. The hunchbacked fairy, half Rosemary's height, waved her flask in Rosemary's direction. "Look, there she be!" A group of fair folk—little dark gnomes, pixies with ragged butterfly wings, and misshapen dwarves—looked.

Rosemary waited. She had, after all, come to speak with this woman, and shuddering would do her no good. Old Peg clumped over the dance grounds, her entourage—including Mad Nan—following in a small mob. She grinned at Rosemary, showing her filthy, half-gone teeth.

"So, you come to your old mither finally."

"I came to hear your story." Her hands tightened on her skirt.

Old Peg's grin widened. "So you don't believe me?"

"With the pastor having bound you to tell the truth?"

Old Peg grimaced and leaned back. Then she peered drunkenly at Rosemary. "Who toll you that?"

Rosemary licked her lips. "No matter. I would still hear your story."

Old Peg contemplated that for a moment, took a gulp from her flask, and shrugged. "Mrs. Whitney was always having parties—and right outside me oak, where me lives." Old Peg snorted. "So I showed her. Switched you for her baby on May Eve."

One, counted Rosemary. She nodded gravely.

The fairy waved her hand in the air. "Was easy. Left the window open, but I didn't hardly need that. . . ."

Rosermary licked her lips; fairies could take children and leave changelings, she knew that, and the details were hardly interesting. "Was that vengeance enough?" she asked, trying to get the woman back on track.

Old Peg snorted again. "Not hardly. She wouldn't hire a good nurse, so her baby kept a-crying, and a-crying. So I showed her. I switched my baby for hers on Midsummer."

Two. Rosemary suppressed the urge to lick her lips again. If Mad Nan sense that Rosemary was counting, the woman would interrupt Old Peg by hook or by crook, and Mad Nan was watching Rosemary intently. "Did that teach her?"

"Not at all! She had her friends down a-picnicking under me own oak, on Lammas! She didn't even get her own baby back in the house then!"

Rosemary clasped her hands together. "Three times!" she exclaimed. She could feel the bewilderment of the men behind her, but she had to get to the bottom of this story.

"Wasn't all. Her baby got around the house and into the brownie's milk—that's mine! I weren't having no woman let her baby interfere with me rights!" Old Peg peered at Rosemary. "I switched the babies on Halloween."

Rosemary nodded gravely. "Four times you switched your baby for Rosemary Whitney. Truly a punishment. Though— did that suffice?" She glanced at Mad Nan; the woman looked puzzled still, but on the verge of furiously driving Rosemary off on general principles. And she had to get to the bottom of this.

No matter how confused Old Peg had been, she might have managed what she was after.

Old Peg nodded and hiccupped. "Let it go at that." Rosemary relaxed. Old Peg spread her hands, the flask still in one. "Couldn't teach her more than that."

"I see," said Rosemary, seriously, and smiled.

Old Peg peered at Rosemary with bleary eyes. "Whatcha smiling at?"

Rosemary's smile deepened, and Old Peg waved her fist at the young woman. "I switched my baby for you four times, Miss Rosemary Whitney!"

Rosemary dismissed her smile and spread her hands. "But, Old Peg," she said seriously, "if you switched your baby for Rosemary Whitney, I am your baby."

Old Peg frowned, her forehead wrinkling in thought, but was unable to figure it out.

"Or," Rosemary added, "I would have been. . . if you hadn't switched us *back*." She smiled more deeply.

Old Peg's face contorted at this modification, but Mad Nan understood; the fairy woman was staring, aghast, at her mother. Rosemary gave her a quick glance and decided to be off before Nan could make trouble. "Thank you for your story."

Old Peg frowned, lowering her hands. "Aren't you staying?"

Rosemary shook her head and hurried off. The men managed to produce lights by the time she reached them, but looked at her in shock. Sir Fitzwilliam appeared on the brink of apoplexy. Rosemary smiled merrily, taking Henry's arm.

"That went neatly enough."

Sir Fitzwilliam shook his head. "Mad, utterly mad," he pronounced.

A scarcely human voice behind them rose in fury. "You utter imbecile!" Mad Nan was berating her mother.

Rosemary glanced back to confirm the fact. She shrugged. "Well, I thought it went neatly enough."

Where There Is Smoke

Marisa woke slowly, finding her face in the middle of something enormous and soft. Confused, she shook her head; she would never have been such a fool as to carry something this useless when they were chasing the Nameless Necromancer. She had not had a pillow like this since she left her apprenticeship, having discovered she did not have the patience to be a wizard.

She rolled over and woke up a little more as she peered at a wall-hanging of a unicorn and a lead-paned window, through which morning sunlight poured. She grimaced, wondering if she were dreaming; it looked like her old room. She rolled over onto her back. Of course, she remembered, blinking, they had caught the necromancer, and she had brought a mysterious tome of his to her old master for his aid in deciphering it. Marisa grinned. Cleaning up the tail ends had a few advantages, when you were in the royal employ.

A boom echoed in the room, shaking the wall-hanging and rattling the panes. Marisa sprang out of bed, startled, and the floor shook a little under her bare feet. She gulped. The noise sounded like thunder, but it definitely sprang from the room below, Jerome's laboratory. She sprang for the door and down the stairs, her brown hair flying behind her.

The oaken door had not budged, but gray smoke, smelling like his alchemy experiments, seeped under it. Marisa grabbed the brass doorknob and yanked.

An enormous cloud of smoke rolled out to greet her. Marisa coughed and tried to peer into the smoke-filled room in spite of her watering eyes. A fit of coughing echoed in the room, and Jerome came slowly into view, his gray robes more than usually scorched and disarrayed. "Lucky my spells of protection work so well." He noticed his former apprentice and nodded to her. "Be careful where you step, my dear; it broke the crucible." He waved his arms in front of him and cleared a gap of air, revealing a table set with a shattered crucible, and an open book with a small lens resting on it.

Marisa briefly noticed the sharp edges of the crucible and felt very aware of her bare feet, but the book caught her attention. "What have you been doing, Master Jerome?" she asked, barely able to keep sharpness out, and respect in, her words.

Jerome beamed and lifted the lens from the tome. "I used one of my translation glasses on the book you brought. It is a book of alchemy—it is not necromancy at all!" He looked down at the crucible. "I tried one of its concoctions." Marisa's eyes narrowed. Jerome held up a hand. "I know, I know. You don't like alchemy."

Marisa spread out her hands. "Alchemy is a way of turning lead into a lion's worth of gold, spending twelve lions in the process."

"I'm down to eight," Jerome said, brightly. "Besides, this is not a transmutation formula. Although it contains only sulfur, charcoal, and saltpeter, it can make things fly through the air!"

Marisa put her hands on her hips. "It nearly," she said, "sent you, and me, and this whole tower, flying through the air."

Jerome tossed one hand in the air in a grandiloquent gesture. "Obviously, it needs more work."

Marisa cocked an eyebrow. "Perhaps breakfast first?"

Jerome took a look around; the smoke had cleared, revealing the scorch marks around the room and the bits of the broken crucible. "I think I'd better clean up first."

Marisa nodded. "I'll see you in the kitchen." She started back up the stairs to dress. He was scatter-brained when I was an apprentice, she thought; but was he this scatter-brained?

A faint noise echoed in the stairwell, drawing her out of her thoughts. She frowned, puzzled: was that a snigger? She looked around, but saw nothing.

The door to the outside stood open in the kitchen, allowing the sunlight and the fresh smells of grasses and wildflowers in. Jerome hunched over the fireplace, stirring up a fire from the banked coals. He nodded to Marisa as she came down.

Marisa, feeling startled at how easily it came back, walked outside to wash her hands. An enchanted jug sat on a wall beside the garden path; tilted on one side, it spilled an endless stream of pure water that ran babbling down the hill. She had forgotten how cold it was and gasped at the first touch, but it came back to her. She looked out over the view, of rows of delicate blue hills beneath a pure cloudless sky, for a long minute before she headed back to the door. What a contrast from hunting the necromancer, she thought with sudden longing for the days of her apprenticeship.

A puff of smoke sprang into the room, and Jerome hopped back, coughing. With watering eyes, he looked at Marisa. "There were eyes in there!" he said, his tone disbelieving.

Marisa looked the cloud of gray wood smoke; she saw nothing untoward, and even the smell was the clear sooty smell of burned wood. She raised her hands and blasted the cloud with a conjured wind; the cloud dissipated. She looked back at Jerome. "Perhaps," she said, "the explosion shook your nerves."

Jerome considered the matter. "Perhaps." He squatted to feed more wood to the fire. Flaxen tongues of fire licked at fuel, greedily.

Marisa sat on one of the stools beside the table. "You're certain that this book is on alchemy, and not necromancy?"

Jerome looked up at her and blinked. "Didn't this morning prove it?"

Marisa's mouth twisted. "The Royal Wizard is not going to be satisfied with that." She tilted her head to one side. "Nor would the king. After all, we found the book in the possession of the Nameless Necromancer, who robbed graves and raised the dead and destroyed entire villages with strange diseases—and he kept it under lock and key."

"I never understand why you went into the royal employ," said Jerome, plaintively. "Hunting down criminals is not a wizard's business." He shook his head. "You learned to cast your spells of fire and cold and sand like lightning, but that's just a matter of practice. Why, you haven't even devised a single spell that could make your name immortal."

Marisa shrugged. "I'm not really a wizard, since I didn't finish my studies, and I haven't the patience to devise spells," she said. "But I must reassure them about the book."

Jerome blinked. "It's all alchemy. I looked it through before I experimented." He went to the cupboard and pulled out the pot. "After all, didn't you say that the chest he kept it in was covered with cobwebs?"

Marisa nodded, slowly.

Jerome beamed. "There you are. He guarded it as a rare work, but it did not help his area of studies."

Marisa nodded again. "It would explain a great deal." She put her elbow to the table to support her chin. "They might even let you keep the book."

Jerome blinked, as if he had not realized he could lose it.

Another explosion rocked the tower. Marisa sighed and laid aside her letter to the Royal Wizard. Jerome was bent on getting the concatenation to work before he lost the book, and she did not think she would get any writing done until he calmed down a little. He was methodical enough to stop to write down his notes; she could write the letter then.

She walked over to the window. The woods and fields spread out over the hills like a pieced quilt in shades of green. She pushed open the window; the white roses climbing over the tower scented the warm breeze. Marisa sat down on the sill, in the sunlight, and began practicing her spells, sending flashes of cold and heat and blasts of air from the palm of her hand. She did not have the aptitude for pure wizardry, but she had shown the Nameless Necromancer that she had plenty of aptitude for some spells! She grinned.

The smell of smoke rose up toward her. Marisa sniffed, frowning. That was not wood smoke. Indeed, it smelled rather like the mess that morning. She looked down, and saw the smoke billowing from the windows. The smell thickened; it was not only the strange mix from the book, but half a dozen other ingredients from Jerome's laboratory.

Marisa leapt to her feet and ran. There hadn't even been an explosion just before, she thought as she ran down the stairs; if Jerome had set the room on fire. Without completing the thought, Marisa yanked open the door.

An almost black cloud of foul-smelling smoke billowed in her face. Coughing, Marisa fell back against the opposite wall. A deep chuckle sounded out of the smoke. Marisa threw her hands up and whipped up a blast of air, dissipating most of the cloud and revealing its core. A black wisp with dull red eyes looked at her, with malice in its eyes. Marisa turned both her hands on the smoke imp, and dissipated it. The imp realized its danger only seconds before it vanished.

Marisa looked into the room. Shattered crockery lay all about, covered with fine layer of soot. Smoke imps billowed in every corner. Fires blossomed on one shelf, glowing pure red, and green, and blue, and an imp that glowed like an orange ember danced about the flames; two more glowing imps clambered over Jerome's books. Jerome himself, covered in dark gray, stood in the center of the room as if frozen.

Marisa turned her winds on him. Black specks fell away at their touch, but the soot cohered and pulled back. A pair of black eyes drifted over Jerome's shoulder to glare at her as the imp tightened its grip.

Not smoke, thought Marisa, but ash. She stepped into the room and brought the full force of the winds to bear. The ash imp clung, but black specks started streaming off it, out the window; she managed to uncover Jerome's face, and the wizard began to choke and sputter. Marisa grinned and turned to blasting off the rest of the ash imp. An ember imp looked up from its book-burning to laugh as if demented; the high, piercing note grated on Marisa's very bones. She set her teeth, resolved that the ember imp was next, and stepped closer to Jerome. The last bits of the ash imp clung to Jerome's arm. Marisa aimed at them, and the eyes dissolved, and the ash lost its grip, going streaming out the window as nothing more than ordinary soot.

Jerome grabbed the table. Marisa turned to the other imps. The ember imp grinned from its chemical flames. Not water, she remembered; water might only make those chemicals float. And sparks could float on the wind. She changed her spell to cold and set its blast on the bookshelves. Frost rimed the books, but the imps dissolved at the touch. Marisa whirled and dispatched the last ember imp, among the chemical fires. The fires puffed out, and the imp stared at her with an open mouth for a second before vanishing like a popped bubble.

Marisa grinned and looked around the room. One of the smoke imps started to advance from its corner, billowing larger. Marisa turned her spell back to wind. The smoke imps could be the hardest, she thought, with their forms already so insubstantial. She set her blast on each one, destroying the first, the second, the third. . . . She turned around, puzzled. There had been four smoke imps in the room, she thought.

Jerome looked at her, and Marisa demanded, "The last imp?" Jerome's eyebrows drew together, and Marisa took a step toward him. "That last smoke imp—where did it go? We can't let it get away."

Jerome lifted one hand to wave it. "I. . .didn't see."

Marisa's mouth set. She ran to the window and looked out. No puff of smoke, as far as she could see. She turned on her heel and ran for the door. Petty as the imps were, they could be dangerous to those not magically inclined. Jerome still looked wrung out, and Marisa's mouth pursed. As well as to those who were, she thought, stepping out into the stairwell. Looking up and down showed no sign of the imp. Smoke rises, she thought and flew up the stairs. She reached the door to her room just in time to see the smoke imp creeping out her window. Marisa blasted it to nothingness from across the room.

The imps didn't stand a chance, Marisa thought, a little smugly; that's the way I blasted the Nameless Necromancer's legions. She remembered Jerome, and the smugness left her. Marisa turned on her heel and started back down.

"My beautiful laboratory," Jerome lamented, as he tried to work a spell of restoration on one of the burned books. Marisa looked around. Scorch marks could not be made out from the layer of soot covering everything. More than half of the bottles had shattered, spilling herbs and salts and strange liquids. The air still stank from the chemical fires.

Marisa shook her head. "What happened?" she demanded.

Jerome looked up, his eyes dark with tragedy. Before he spoke, something hissed. Marisa turned to see a little cloud of steam forming in midair. She barely made out the electric blue eyes before she whipped out a blast of cold against the steam imp. A cloud of ice crystals formed and fell to the floor.

Marisa turned back to Jerome and repeated herself. "What. Happened."

Jerome swallowed. "The compound, it appears, opened a rift to the dimension of fire." He swallowed again. "Perhaps it was the stuff's fiery nature; perhaps it just opens rifts, and chanced upon that world." He muttered a wizard-sight spell and looked about to test his theory.

Marisa looked about, aghast. She muttered a wizard-sight spell of her own, looked for magic about the room, and froze as she saw fiery glittering all about.

"When the fire elementals see the rift, some of them hop through." Jerome's mouth pursed.

"It must have been a smoke imp downstairs, in the kitchen," Marisa said. She felt numb.

Jerome's head bobbed. "Then, just now, a whole group noticed." His mouth pursed. "Plus, of course, the rifts are larger. Just as well it happened now. If they hadn't noticed until later, and came through then, I might not have realized what the cause was." Marisa cringed at the thought; Jerome would not have lived to realize if she had left by then. Jerome, looking almost recovered, looked about critically. His eyes narrowed as he concentrated. "There aren't any rifts outside this room."

"But there's nothing to keep things larger than those imps out," Marisa said. Jerome nodded. "There's nothing to keep a salamander out!" she bellowed.

Jerome's eyes grew large. Marisa took a step toward him, almost menacing. "Close the rifts again," she ordered.

"I can't close them," he said. "Only the elementals can."

Marisa choked. Her hands clenched and unclenched. Jerome turned back to his ruined books, and Marisa forced herself to take a deep breath. She was the only royal representative for several day's journey; it was her duty to investigate, even if she had gone into the job because there was little else for a half-trained wizard.

"Well," she said, quietly, but Jerome looked up. "If they can close it, we must make them want to." Her eyes narrowed. "They do not like cold, but I do not think my spell is large enough." Her eyes went to the ruined chemicals, which she had not doused with water, and her thoughts rambled off to just before breakfast. "They do not like water, and since the dimension burns of its own nature, we need not worry about floating chemicals."

Jerome tilted his head to one side to peer at her. "Your water spell is better than your cold?"

Marisa grinned. "No. But there is the bottomless jug of water. If we only make the room waterproof, we can flood it, and inspire the elementals to seal it off."

"My poor laboratory! It's already been burned!"

Marisa turned on him, her lips drawing back from her teeth. "The next ash imp could make it a matter of indifference to you, Jerome."

Jerome bobbed his head sadly and said, "We'll have to salvage what we can, first."

"I," said Marisa, imperiously, "have to keep watch for further imps." Jerome did not argue. As he starting moving things out, Marisa realized that for the first time, she had not addressed him as Master Jerome.

Marisa sat in the hole in her room's floor, next to the jug. Its water flowed in a smooth cascade down into the laboratory, where it already reached the knee-high. The flood lapped higher and reached the first rift. Water started to flow in, and a hiss arose. She looked at it narrowly to make sure it was not a steam imp.

"Hum," said Jerome. Marisa glanced over to see her old teacher with his nose in the book that had started all the trouble.

"I wonder," said the wizard, looking up, "if other compounds would open to other worlds, or if fire, being the most active, is the only one."

Marisa gave him a look.

Jerome blinked. "Why, my dear, you learned that much alchemy." He closed the book, keeping his finger in his place. "The ignorant refer to the four elements, as if they were the building blocks. No, fire, air, water, and earth are the four forms that matter takes, based on the heat inside them. Fire is the hottest and hence the most active. . . ."

Marisa stopped listening. After he nearly died unleashing a horror on the world, he would go and think. . .she choked off that thought, decided to risk the imps, and rose to her feet to take the book from Jerome. He blinked at her in surprise.

"The Nameless Necromancer himself kept this book under lock and key, and never touched it. Now I know why." Marisa drew a deep breath, surprised at the fury in her voice. She rose to her full height and declared, "Some magics were too foul even for him." She stalked back to the hole. The Royal Wizard would not mind her disposing of the book, it being so dangerous. She looked down and saw that most of the rifts were still open. She got down on her knees, took careful aim, and shot the book into one. It burst into orange flame. She watched it every second until the book crumpled into ashes at the mouth of the rift. Marisa gave it a critical eye, and send a wind down to stir up the ashes.

"A pity," said Jerome, mournfully. "It had this recipe with nitric acid and glycerin that looked interesting."

Marisa gave him a baneful glance. "I would suggest," she said, her voice very low, "that you don't even think of trying it."

Jerome looked taken aback, but did not argue.

The Magic of the Lost God

The campfire glowed in the entrance of the cave where they camped. Alice Ladybird looked uneasily at the walls of the Egyptian tomb. The light flickered over the hieroglyphics and the painting of workers reaping the harvest. Her stepsister might grub through sand to find bits of mummy without a twinge, and talk of how the natives wanted nothing so much as a rich tomb to plunder, but Alice still felt uneasy.

Alice looked back to the fire where her mother and stepfather sat. She decided, abruptly, that Veronica had a good idea in taking a moonlight walk. She walked to the entrance and looked out at the silvered sand. The moon's flat white light spread out without a cloud to dim it. Her hand rested on the entrance for a second. She had not dreamed what it would mean, when her mother declared she was marrying a widower with a daughter. The then Cordelia Ladybird had not even mentioned that Edward Black was an Egyptologist—though that had affected Alice more than anything else. She started to walk.

A sound broke into her thoughts. A low voice came over the dunes, intoning something over and over. Alice frowned; she recognized Veronica's voice, but not what she said; Veronica was reciting, "Abdom. Abdom. Abdom."

Alice slowly walked around the dune, ready to freeze at any second, and saw Veronica, sitting cross-legged and looking at papers in front of her—fortunately with her back to her stepsister.

Veronica stopped and looked up, looking sternly on the air a yard ahead of her. "I have given you your name," she said, fiercely. "I have given you the power you have not had in three millennia. Give me the love of Captain James Miller."

Alice blinked. They had met Captain Miller at his regiment earlier in the month. She gave her stepsister a sidelong glance. Captain Miller was a handsome man, about thirty-five, of independent means. She licked her lips; the captain was also already engaged to be married.

The air in front of Veronica shimmered in the moonlight. Alice's breath caught. A voice as dry as sand came out of the air. "He is faithful to his love."

A cold smile twitched Veronica's lips. "Would I want the love of one who would be unfaithful?"

"It will not be easy," the voice said. "Much power is needed to win faithful love." Silence reigned for a second. Veronica looked at the haze with cold eyes. The voice added, "I will need my name. Many times."

Alice, scarcely breathing, began to carefully work her way back to the camp. Veronica seemed bent on her bargaining, but Alice did not want to attract her attention.

The evening's cool damp air came in off the Nile and slipped through the windows into the ballroom. Alice stood against the wall, watching the waltz. Other dancers swirled through her vision, but she watched one handsome pair, a woman in elegant pale green gown, and a officer in his regimentals, the light shining on her red hair and his chestnut brown. A smug smile hovered on Veronica's face; Captain Miller looked down at her with an adoring but puzzled expression.

Alice's eyes drifted across the ballroom to where Isabelle Higgins stood among the captain's messmates, trying to flirt. Miss Higgins wore a blue gown, the finest in the room, and her blond hair was arranged to perfection, but her blue eyes, with plaintive shadows, kept drifting back across the ballroom to her fiance. Alice's mouth tightened. Captain Miller had not even asked Miss Higgins for a dance, or noticed her flirting.

Alice's eyes fell. Only minutes after she had returned to camp, Veronica had followed her. Apparently, her stepsister had brought her haggling to a close quickly.

"May I have this dance, Miss Ladybird?"

Alice turned quickly, surprise by the apparition of one of the captains at her shoulder. "Oh, no, thank you, but I'm just too tired now," she said. The captain looked disappointed, but with thoughts of Veronica flooding her mind, Alice did not trust herself not to step all over her partner's feet.

"Perhaps some punch to refresh you," said Captain—Arthbut, Alice remembered.

Alice made herself smile. "Why, that would be delightful," she declared. She accepted Arthbut's arm. Perhaps it would distract her from Veronica, since she could do nothing about her stepsister anyway.

Veronica's laugh rang across the ballroom. Alice wondered, with a touch of malice that surprised her, if her stepsister had thought of breach of promise suits. Miss Higgins, if rumor told the truth, had enough spirit to fight once the shock wore off.

Alice drowsed a little in bed, wondering why the sun had to get up so early in the morning. She yawned and almost resolved to return to sleep.

She heard Veronica move in the bedroom next to her, and then her stepsister's shuffling papers. Alice woke completely, and licked her lips. She got slowly out of bed and crept closer to the wall, laying her ear against it.

The walls muffled the words, but Alice could make them out. "Abdom," said her stepsister, "I require more. You shall have your name if you fulfill it."

The dry voice barely reached the wall. "You promised my name for the love of Captain Miller."

Alice could almost see Veronica's dismissing gesture. "I need more. Turn the love of Isabelle Higgins away from him."

After a second, the voice, still dry but almost petulant, said, "You bargained for the heart of Captain Miller."

Her tone mocking, Veronica said, "What, can you not?"

The voice grew dry again. "I have changed the heart of many a man and woman now dust. I have let no scruple bind me. I have kept my bargains, and I have kept this one."

The papers rustled as if Veronica lifted something from them. "I have the last inscription of your name," Veronica said, her voice low and threatening.

The noon sunlight dazzled outside the house. Alice sat on the porch, leaning back in the wicker chair. One of Edward Black's books on Egypt sat in her lap, and in spite of the heat, she read intently about the parchments. The book had one or two comments about magical intent, but no detail. Her fingers tightened on the page in frustration, crinkling it. As if a book would easily lay out for her all she needed to defeat Veronica's plans! Alice bit her lip. Rumor said that Miss Higgins had broken her engagement and seemed not to care, and Veronica herself had talked of Captain Miller and, with more pleasure, of his rich father.

Mr. Black's jovial voice rang out over the porch. "Why, Alice, are you finding the study of Egypt interesting?" He came up beside her chair. "I know you did not, at first."

Alice turned her eyes demurely down to the book. "It grows more—intriguing," she said. She looked up. "It talks about magical writings; how did the Egyptians use them?"

Mr. Black sat in the nearest chair and leaned back. "Why, they held that words have power, especially names. By repeating someone's name, whether aloud or in writing, you gave him power. By eradicating a name...." His hand closed on air. "You eradicated him." Silence reigned for a second. "Pharaohs were known to try to strike their enemies' names from every inscription where they occurred, for that very reason."

Alice frowned, her forehead creasing. "If, on the other hand, you wanted magical power," she thought aloud, "you would have someone repeat your name."

The man smiled. "No, you would repeat a god's name, and have him work magic on your behalf because of the power you gave him." His tone grew more ponderous, like a university lecture. "The magicians favored more obscure gods, who were more grateful for such power."

Alice licked her lips. "How could any being who could use a man's help do more than what the man himself could do?" she asked, tentatively.

His smile deepened. "There," he declared, "you have hit on the essential absurdity of the whole system." He leaned back. "Not that it matters to us; the gods of ancient Egypt could hardly speak English."

Alice said nothing. Much though he loved her mother, it would not trouble Edward Black much to lock up his stepdaughter as a lunatic.

Alice let her hand rest against the porch wall. "I really think that the dazzle would make my headache worse," she said. She glanced sidelong through her eyelashes at her mother.

Cordelia Black shrugged as she pulled on her gloves. "You should have been more careful about wearing a hat," she said, faintly rebuking. She left for the carriage, where Veronica already waited. Alice, her eyes grave, watched the carriage leave and turned back inside.

In the kitchen the cook said something, the noise if not the meaning reaching through the wall, and the maid laughed. Alice started up the stairs, glancing at the kitchen door now and then until she reached the landing. The servants seemed bent on their chatter. Alice drew a deep breath and hurried down the hall. She pulled open the door to Veronica's room and stepped within.

One of Veronica's dress sprawled over the chair. A half-open drawer revealed her parchments, with a hieroglyphic-covered piece of pottery sitting on it. Alice, feeling a little chilly, looked at the amulet without touching it and translated the forms into their sounds. She spelled out "Abdom" and felt even colder: now she had no excuse. Carefully, she pulled the drawer open and took out the amulet. The pottery shard seemed as bland as any piece she had ever seen. Her hand tightened about it as she remembered that Veronica had wrought no magic to speak with the god again.

"Abdom," Alice said.

The air shimmered like a mirage. "You are not her," said the god, his voice as dry as a desert wind.

Alice gulped, wondering what the god could do with her name. Do not tell him it, she decided. She gave the haze another look and resolved not to give it her stepsister's, either. "I am not. I bargain for myself." The hieroglyphics pressed into her hand as her grip tightened.

After a second of silence, the god said, "What do you bargain for?"

Alice answered promptly: "That you break the spells you cast on Captain Miller and Miss Higgins. That you take the knowledge from—her mind, who bargained for you for the spells on Captain Miller and Miss Higgins—that you take from her the knowledge of how to cast such spells."

Silence reigned for a long minute. The god's voice grew menacing when he spoke again: "What will you give for this?"

Alice lifted her hand. "I have the last inscription of your name," she said.

A breeze swirled the curtains. Alice did not, quite, think that the god had done it, but she glanced uneasily at it.

The god's voice was flat. "She gave me my name."

"No one will give you your name again if I destroy this," Alice said, harshly. She remembered its brag of changing hearts and wondered if she could leave such a plague to the future, but she had no other way to free the captain and Miss Higgins.

After a minute, the god spoke. "I will do it."

Alice lifted her head. "When?"

The shimmer rippled. "I have done it."

Alice nodded, once. She lay the amulet back down on the chest and looked at the parchments. "I ought to destroy these," she said, thinking aloud.

"Oh, do not." The voice grew as coaxing as its dryness would permit. "Only those spells will let you summon up me, and I can give you great power."

Alice's mouth tightened. She had not promised to spare the parchments. She started to pick up the parchments.

"Do not," the god said, fiercely, and Alice felt heat strike her like a blow. She gave the shimmer a baneful glance, and the god's voice deepened. "Do not!" She dragged in a deep breath, and the air seared her lungs.

Alice grabbed the handiest thing and hurled it blindly at the voice. She heard a faint sound of breaking pottery and stood in a suddenly empty room. She staggered back, catching herself on the bureau; the parchments crackled in her hand against the wood. The cracked clay lay opposite, against the wall. Alice's mouth twisted. She remembered that the god had only taken her stepsister's knowledge of how to work the magic, not her will. Alice walked across the room to grind the amulet under her heel before she burned the parchments.

Veronica sat in the corner of the ballroom and sulked. Alice ignored her. Veronica had worried Edward and Cordelia ever since that afternoon, when Veronica had returned from the call with a look of settled fury on her face.

Alice had other worries. Her eyes went to the man in the opposite corner of the ballroom, watching Isabelle Higgins dance with Captain Arthbut. Miss Higgins laughed merrily. Alice looked away; Miss Higgins had not cast a single glance at Captain Miller all evening. The god might have freed her heart, but he had not cured her wounded vanity.

Alice's eyes half-closed, her eyelashes veiling them. Not, she conceded judiciously, that Miss Higgins ought to put up with that kind of treatment; even if the captain had known the truth, Miss Higgins would laugh in his face at such an outlandish excuse. Alice's eyes returned to Captain Miller.

Marrying Veronica would have made him more miserable, Alice reminded herself, and not long ago she thought that she could have done nothing at all. Suddenly, the ballroom felt very close. Alice gathered her skirts and hurried outside, murmuring brief excuses to her acquaintances. One matron took her sleeve. "You look very pale, Miss Ladybird," Mrs. Carstairs said.

Alice nodded. "I thought the night air." She glanced at the veranda's door, and the matron nodded and let her go. She started to talk with her companions again: "Really, Captain Miller acted so very badly toward her, I wouldn't...."

Alice hurried out into the cooler air that smelled of the Nile. She drew in a deep breath and looked out into the darkness. The ballroom cast squares of light on the veranda, but beyond that only the half moon and the stars shone. The Nile's ripples now and then appeared, carrying a silver reflection. Alice sighed, watching them.

The door opened again, and a man stood shadowed against it. Alice glanced over while he was still outlined against the lights, and recognized Captain Miller. She drew back. The man would hardly want to see her.

His head jerked around at the movement. "Excuse me, madam."

"There's plenty of room for two, if you want a breath of fresh air," Alice said. He frowned a little, as if he recognized her voice, and leaned on the railing to stare out at the dark waters. After a minute, she said, "It's certainly very close in the ballroom."

Captain Miller grunted his agreement. He pushed off the railing and said, "And, of course, there's all the gossiping matrons." His mouth set. Alice tilted her head to one side. "Do not look so inquiring, Miss Ladybird; I can not tell you how I lost my head over your sister."

Alice shrugged. "She can have that effect." She looked at Captain Miller and was glad that Veronica started to sulk once her spell broke; if her stepsister had continued to pursue him, Captain Miller might have felt that he was honor-bound to her.

Captain Miller looked at her strangely. Alice lifted her head, realizing that the captain probably thought she had seen more of these affairs; she said, coolly, "It is probably best to put the whole affair aside."

Captain Miller flinched. "Miss Higgins," he said, "has already put the whole affair aside."

Alice spread her hands. "There are other ladies at the ball," she said, dryly. "You need not pledge your heart, but you ought not to mope in the corner. Activity is the best cure for a broken heart."

Captain Miller gave her a strange look. "May I have the next dance?"

Alice stood with her mouth open for a second. "Yes, certainly," she said, wondering if the captain thought she had been angling for the dance.

Mrs. Carstairs drew Alice aside by the punch bowl, casting a wary glance at Captain Miller. "I must warn you," she said, her voice low. "You saw how he cast your sister aside, but perhaps you did not know that he was engaged to Miss Higgins before your family arrived."

Alice cast her eyes down, not quite willing to tell Mrs. Carstairs that she had promised Captain Miller two more dances. One had been quite enough to confirm that Veronica's excellent taste.

"Oh, you girls! You would ruin your life without a second thought!" Mrs. Carstairs's excellent advice poured out as Alice sipped her punch and looked across the room. Her eyebrows went up. Her stepsister, her cheeks flushed, glared at Alice with a fury greater than the afternoon when she lost her magic.

Alice turned away. A minute later, she heard Veronica at her shoulder. "You little sneak, do you think you will be able to catch him?" Alice looked over her shoulder at her stepsister. Veronica spat, "You haven't a twopence to your name."

Alice shrugged again. "You have not seemed much interested in him for the last week," she said, lazily. She smiled a little. This part of foiling Veronica was much more pleasant than the first, she thought.

Isabelle and the Siren

A wordless melody drifted sweetly into the white-washed room with the morning sunlight. Isabelle lay in bed, contemplating the ceiling. I should have stayed in the city, she thought; my melancholia made it hard to do anything, but out here, convalescing, with nothing that has to be done by a given time— why, I do nothing. A sea breeze tugged at the white bed-hangings. Isabelle wrinkled her nose. Even get up.

Outside she heard the townsfolk moving toward something outside the town (perhaps toward the music, but she could not rouse the concentration to tell, or the energy to care). Thoughts floated vaguely through her mind, as detached as if they had no connection to her: about how all the townsfolk would think her a perfect sluggard, taking two hours to get up. She had managed to get up in the city. Then, when she had heard two townsfolk talking about how the Professor of Rhetoric—her own father— had debated Satan for the title Prince of Lies, and won, she had not only not defended her father, she had not cared. She rolled over. Still didn't, she thought.

She forced the thoughts away. I have to get up, she resolved. Now.

Isabelle lay in bed, unmoving, over an hour while the music faded away. She vaguely registered that she could not hear the townsfolk, which was unlike them. Most of the fishermen went out to sea, but the townsfolk had shops and kitchen gardens, and she had gotten thoroughly familiar with the noises of morning, since she had not gotten up early once in the two weeks she had spent in the town.

Isabelle sighed. There were times when she could not figure out not only how she had gotten herself a scholarship in magical zoology, but how she had gotten herself to the town. Professor Arthurson may have suggested that she be sent out to the countryside, like a sickly baby with its wetnurse, but she had made the arrangements.

I have to get up, Isabelle thought again, and somewhat to her own surprise, found herself getting up. Having done so, she managed to keep going, to walk toward the window, pick up her dressing gown, and look out the window as she put it on.

The square outside was completely empty. The store stood open, but Mistress Agatha did not stand behind its counter. The clapboard houses stood silent among the dunes. Down the street, an open door swung in the wind, and over the dunes, the sea, empty of boats, glittered in the sunlight. A thin, piercing cry echoed from the house next to her. Isabelle turned her face toward it as the baby's crying went on and on. She frowned: Kate might aggravate her with perpetual chatter but would never let her daughter cry like that.

Isabelle sighed and headed for the stairs. Her hand rested loosely on the railing as she walked downstairs. "Angel of God," she thought, "my guardian dear, to whom His love commits me here, ever this day be by my side, to watch, to lead, to guard, to guide." The prayer rattled itself off mechanically, without engaging her mind. She reminded herself, dutifully, that she would need all the leading and guiding she could get, but roused no enthusiasm in herself; she could not even manage curiosity at what had stolen the townsfolk away—or shock at her inability to feel it.

She opened the front door. A sea breeze came in to pull at her pale brown hair and tug at her sky blue dressing gown. Isabelle swallowed and wondered if the music earlier had been responsible—strange music to be heard in this worthy if dull town. She walked down the street, reminding herself again that while she had not completed her studies, she had been a promising zoologist—had even planned to write a book before she was graduated. Besides, something had to be done, however black her mood. She forced herself to look about. The clapboard houses stood in rows, painted pale yellows and blues and grays, neat and respectable, except for the number of doors swinging open.

Music came floating through the air, sweet and faintly familiar from the morning. Isabelle stopped at the edge of town, listening to the alien notes and slowly matching them to her studies. A siren sang there: a humanoid winged beast, a carrion eater that made its own carrion. She glanced over the dunes. The siren was inhuman and unintelligent, but dangerous; even to her, the music sounded attractive.

Isabelle turned and walked back into the town. When Professor Arthurson had babbled about the town as a perfect, quiet place for convalescence, she had complied more out of being too listless to argue than of thinking it would do her any good, but she had not thought something like this would happen. Why, Arthurson had cited that nothing ever happened here, that its nominal duke had never been troubled by it since the end of the Viking raids, as its chief attraction. She glanced over her shoulder, noting that the seclusion would also give shelter to monsters.

The music came after her, growing more alluring. The siren must have seen her, Isabelle realized as she reached the house where she rented the room; it could have, since its eyes were like an eagle's, and it would eagerly draw more prey. Isabelle swallowed. The siren might even be able to draw her, melancholia or no melancholia, if its song grew alluring enough.

She walked into the kitchen and looked around. Wax, she thought, remembering Ulysses. She started to look through Mistress Catherine's cabinets.

The song wound its way into the house, and Isabelle felt a tug on herself, a desire to go, such as she had not felt for months, ever since these melancholia had fallen on her. She looked down into the last drawer she had opened, and saw a butcher's cleaver. The music called, more and more sweetly; her desire to follow was not strong, but it was growing. Isabelle drew a deep breath. I must pick up this knife, especially since I can't find any wax, she sternly told herself, even if I can find no interest in doing so; at the very least, I must think of the townsfolk. She reached down, picked it up, and breathed a deep sigh of relief, flexing her fingers around this unexpected victory.

The siren sang on. Isabelle decided, gravely, that she had best go before the song numbed her mind, while she could still resist. She turned and walked out of the house, down the street, and out toward the song.

The sunlight shone over the beige sand and the rippling sea. Isabelle walked on through the dune grass and the wild roses, noticing the trampled grass and the footprints in the sand that showed she was following the townsfolk. The song grew no more alluring, but it tugged on her like a fisherman's line.

Isabelle looked over the cove. Ahead the beach rose up into a rocky pile, and on the other side, there was a cliff face, and there the bent grass and footsteps in the sand marked the townsfolk' path. Isabelle's mouth pursed. Which would, indeed, be the way the siren would want them to go.

Not that way, then, Isabelle thought, setting her will as if she were resolving to get up. She started to walk along the water's edge, skirting the rocks. The song faltered for a second, and grew more enticing. Isabelle bit her lip. The lure was stronger than the blackest of her moods; she could not stop herself from going forward.

But I can, she told herself, not go over the cliff. Even when I wanted to kill myself, and had, in my lighter moods, the will power to do, I did not. Therefore I *can* go around. Her knees smashed against a boulder, blinding in pain; Isabelle caught herself against the rock. This is not, she thought with grim humor, what I meant when I said I would like to be rid of my melancholia.

She came around the cliff-face. Spread across the rocks at the bottom of the cliff were the townsfolk, men, women, and children, broken against the stone; some of them had crawled on, tearing their wrecked bodies against the stones. One of them still tried to pull herself on, toward the siren; her legs were shattered, but her bloody hands dug into the sands to pull her toward the song.

Not all dead yet, then, Isabelle thought, recognized Kate, and felt her heart grow cold at the sight of the woman's glazed eyes. Her eyes went past them—she could do nothing for them while the siren lived, she reminded herself. Up on the slope, on the other side, stood the siren herself.

A figure like a slender woman stood there; blue feathers instead of hair fell from her head, blue down covered her body, and two great wings spread from her back. Her face was pale and innocent as the wondrous music bubbled from her lips; she could be taken for human. Isabelle, her hand tightening on the cleaver, walked slowly toward the siren, picking her way through the broken rocks. She could not have stopped walking; the song's charm would not have let her. Her hand shook a little as she prayed that the charm would let her strike.

The siren's soulless eyes looked at Isabelle; they were brown, enormous, and as placid as a cow's. The woman drew in a sharp breath, knowing she could never take the siren for human. A faint expression of astonishment crossed the siren's face, but it shrugged the emotion off. Its hands came up, long black claws spreading from them. Isabelle lifted her cleaver; the siren did not notice as it stepped forward to strike down its prey.

Isabelle struck. The cleaver sliced into the siren's unprotected side. Its song choked off into a cry of pain. Blood gouted, again and again as its heart beat. The siren stepped back, astonishment on its face, and Isabelle dodged to one side as it fell. The flow of blood slackened. The siren's eyes stared blankly at the sky.

"Mistress Isabelle!" A pain-filled voice rose over the sand. Isabelle turned to see Kate raising her hand again. The woman's eyes were human again, but Isabelle bit her lip, surveying the wreckage of the bodies. She raised her voice: "I will do what I can; first I must see how many of you still live."

Kate sank back, nodding weakly, and Isabelle started to look over the bodies. The nearest one to her was dead, but the young man next still breathed, however shallowly; blood oozed from his side. She went through the bodies, cataloging, and stopped by the worst injured living—a boy of twelve, with blood seeping from his body. It would be a long time to work through them all. She pushed back hair from her face. And then there was getting them to shelter and getting help. She closed her eyes briefly, and reminded herself that she had learned the spell to communicate across leagues, even if she had forgotten it in her zoology studies. She could reconstruct it, and the duke, if he had had no dealings with this part of his duchy for years, owned them a great deal of protection and aid for their taxes.

A gull cried, overhead. Isabelle reached for the shirt to tear it into bandages. Her hands froze on the cloth.

I'm not, she realized, having any difficulty helping them— nothing like even getting up. She glanced back at the siren's body. It had been earlier, she realized; she had felt horrified when she had first seen the bodies.

A grim laugh sprang to her lips, but Isabelle managed to choke it down into an unrecognizable bark. She looked around the ruined bodies, and thought that it would never be accepted as a cure. She finished binding the boy's injuries and moved on.

A crow had come to peck at the siren's body. Isabelle grimaced and hurried her bandaging. She could already hear Professor Arthurson's lament at the loss of so valuable a specimen, but she had gained enough lore about the siren to see her to a professorship.

An old man started to cough up blood. Isabelle's mouth set, and she drew her mouth back to the present. Treat all the injured, perhaps get them to shelter, she started to list, work out the spell. She almost flinched away from the length of the list, but stiffened her resolve: it did not feel as hard as getting up had been that morning, and she had managed that.

Crow Curse

Fritha stood by the edge of the pond, looking out over the rushes and the waters reflecting the half-full moon, and sulked. "It wasn't theft," she thought; "the hermit had said to take the books after he died." Fritha scowled, tossing back her dark brown curls from her pale, square face. "The books hadn't been on his body, anyway."

The moon climbed a little higher, and the hour came. Fritha cawed and spread her black wings. She flew to perch on the nearest bush. "Maybe," she thought, bleakly, "Isobel had a point; the wizard who had laid the curse, all those generations ago, might, God willing, decide they had learned to not steal from the bodies of the dead—but something that looked like stealing would change his mind."

The rest of the murder lifted up, cawing. Fritha glared at them. Off to steal all the seed Farmer William had planted, she thought in disgust; Lord have mercy on us all. She flew off. The wizard had not reappeared in seven generations, and while wizards lived long lives, they did not live that long. And neither Isobel nor any other of the crow folk could cast the first stone about theft.

Curses on Simon, anyway, Fritha thought, settling on a dead tree; it was his fault his family was cursed, and he was so old that he had only lived with the curse a couple of years. Fritha ruffled her feathers and wished she could leave the marsh, but where in the world could she go? One of their foolish young men had seduced a woman in the nearest village. His baby had been beaten to death after the first time he changed.

Golden light burst over the horizon. Fritha squawked, lifting off from her perch. Smoke started to rise where the light had come, obscuring the stars behind it. Fritha started to fly back, but further bursts of light caught her attention. Two figures, little more than doll-size at this distance, appeared in the middle of the light, floating over the tree-tops. The crow flew in low, glancing up now and then. Wizards, Fritha thought, and her mind conjured up a dream, of one of the wizards having laid the curse, and now she could charge in and save him, and get the curse lifted. That would show Isobel.

A burst of scarlet light seared the ground next to her, and smoke thickly rose. Fritha flitted back. A dream, of course, she thought. These strange beings lived in another world, and needed no aid from human or crow.

Fritha perched to watch the fight. The bursts grew more and more fierce, ranging through every color of the rainbow. Below them, fires sprung up, and some of the bursts, going astray, made the earth shake.

One wizard threw out his arms, and with a final burst of light, struck down the other wizard. The light about the other one dimmed, and vanished; in the glow from the first wizard, Fritha could see him sinking like a leaf from a tree, but he fell past that light, and vanished. His fall had been so convoluted that he could go anywhere after that.

The other wizard laughed, the noise suddenly so loud that the marsh grass quaked beneath it. "Too late, too late, little Oliver! Nothing you and your family can do save you!"

Fritha shrank back and looked the fires. The fight could have lasted an hour, she realized, and nearly panicked. Without attention to the surviving wizard, she flew to the ground, just barely making it before her form shifted again. That had cutting it too close, Fritha scolded herself as she hurried through the marsh; she ought to not let even fighting wizards distract her. She glanced over her shoulder. The surviving wizard had lowered himself just over the height of the marsh grass. The light around him cast fierce shadows as he peered over the water and land. Fritha turned away, before he could find her.

"Girl!" called a voice, sounding like a man at the last of his strength.

Fritha froze. The wizard could not have fallen this far, she thought, even with that convoluted path.

"Girl, I know you hear me," said the wizard. "Please, I beg you, do not turn away."

What, wondered Fritha, could make a wizard beg for help? She turned to face him. A gray-bearded man lay against a tuffet of marsh grass. His elaborate robe glittered a little in the moonlight, except where blood caked over the cloth. He held out his hand; a ring glittered on it.

"Please, take the ring," he said. "Keep it from William. Give my brother it, when he comes." He coughed.

He could die before I take it, Fritha thought. To take from the bodies of the dead...she stared blankly at the ring.

The wizard's thin, haggard face worked. "He will destroy us," he pled. "All my family—for no crime but thwarting him." His voice faded as he spoke, and at his last word, his head rolled back.

Taking from the bodies of the dead, Fritha thought uneasily. She crept closed to the body and looked up at the searching wizard, whose square face was set in lines of fury.

His voice boomed out again: "How dare you and yours question me? I have shown you what weaklings you are!"

If that man, thought Fritha, laid the curse, it will never get lifted.

The ring glittered in her palm. Fritha tucked the ring away and hurried through the marsh again. The other wizard was moving and and forth over the waters, and now she had more reason not to be found. She splashed through the shallow waters of a stream and climbed the other bank.

Bess's voice carried out of the shadows. "Fritha! What happened here?"

Fritha turned sharply. Half a dozen—a dozen—of the crow folk stood on the opposite bank, among the bushes on the rise of land, and stared at the wizard. Fritha drew in a long breath. "Two wizards were fighting. One of them is down." She gestured at the other. "He's looking for him, I think."

"Is he?" Bess looked after him. "How interesting." She started down the bank.

"Bess!" Fritha said sharply. "If he sees you..."

Bess looked over her shoulder and laughed. "He's looking for a wizard," she said. "Not a poor girl of the crow folk."

Fritha bit her lip. Bess had been the only other child of the crow folk who let the hermit teach her letters, but they did not get along. "Foolish," muttered Todd behind her.

"Who's going to stop her?" said someone else. A murmur of agreement ran through the crow folk. Fritha's shoulders slumped as she nodded in reluctant agreement; she had never been able to stop Bess from any folly. The crow folk started to pull back; Fritha could not help glancing over her shoulder as the wizard drew nearer and nearer the body. She was barely able to keep her hand from going to the pouch with the ring; it felt like an enormous weight on her belt.

Minutes later, Bess came splashing after them. "I was right," she said, half-laughing. "He was only interested in the body." The crow folk looked at her, and she tossed her head. "Said someone else must have been there first." Her eyes bright, she glanced over at Fritha. "He was *angry*."

Fritha collected her wits and snorted. "Unless it fell out over the marsh," she said.

"He'll never find it then," Todd said. Bess's expression fell a little as she agreed. Fritha kept her face set, but her heart started to beat faster. Even if Bess wanted to denounce her, she had no evidence, she reminded herself, but her heart did not slow.

Fritha sat down at the table for her breakfast one morning two weeks later. Her father did not look up from his porridge. "The fires the wizards set have burnt out," he said to his wife. "Or so Ned says. I'm going fishing over there today."

His wife bobbed her head. "'Cept that Meg said that her Polly saw the wizards again," she said, without turning from the fire. "No sense in being where they are."

Fritha wondered if one of the wizards were the dead one's brother. She bolted her porridge and announced, "I'll go weed the garden." Her father mumbled something. Fritha hurried from the room into the chilly morning air. The mist lay thickly over the marsh, but half a dozen women already sat on their thresholds, patching clothing or knitting socks. The old road, built over a century ago, when the queen consort had been born in the county, led into the marsh, but mist hid it after a few paces. Fritha went around back and got down on her knees to weed, but she looked out over the marsh for any sign of the wizards.

As if, she scolded herself a second later, she could see anything through the mist. She bent down over the plants and the dark earth and began to weed. The cold and damp seeped through her skirts, and Fritha weeded faster, trying to warm herself.

A ruckus rose out of the swamp, a confusion of quacking and honking, and Fritha looked quickly up. The air filled with ducks and geese over one pool, but she saw nothing more than their flight. Her mouth twisted as she looked back down. Any number of boys from the village might have tried to catch one, and set them off, she told herself; there was no clue that the wizards had been the cause.

In spite of herself, Fritha glanced back at the waterfowl. Something flashed in the whiteness of the mist. Fritha froze.

"Look at that!" shouted a child's shrill voice. "Is that what you saw, Todd?"

Burst of yellow lit up the mist from with and melted it away more quickly than the sun. The crow folk piled out of their cottages, shouting and exclaiming. "Maybe the wizard's going to lift the curse!" one hopeful said, and they all chattered about the possibility.

Fritha sat back on her heels but could not move any further. Her legs felt very cold, but the pouch with the ring weighed heavily against her thigh; there had been times, now and then, in the last weeks where she could forget it (though she had not dared take it off), but now, she had to get rid of it. "I promised the wizard," she murmured, "and he was dying, too." She looked at the wizards fighting in the mists. How on earth could she tell which one was the brother, and which the foe, at this range? If she could, how could she catch the brother's attention?

Fritha got slowly to her feet, her legs complaining of her long kneeling. She shook them out, not taking her eyes from the fight. Every one of the crow folk stood in the street, exclaiming fear of the wizard, or hope for the lifting of the curse. Her fingers traced the ring in her pouch. Lord help me, she thought.

"Everyone back!" Isobel's voice rose the din. The old woman looked banefully around the crowd. "Back, away from the fight. Stop your staring! If he lifts the curse, 'twill do you no good if you die first."

The crow folk grumbled but obeyed. Fritha bit her lip, guessing this would be her only change to be rid of the ring. She stepped closer to the cottage, hiding beneath the thatch, as the crow folk pulled back, and hurried the other way.

Light exploded from the air, illuminating the whole marsh; Fritha threw up an arm to protect her eyes, but it burned away the mist and revealed a third figure, floating barely above the height of the water. Fritha ducked down, low among the grass, and scurried toward him: a servant, a kinsman, someone who could reach the fighting wizards.

A young man, not ten years older than Fritha, watched the wizards with narrowed eyes. His thin, sharp face reminded her of the dead wizard, far more than the survivor. Fritha frowned, wondering how to tell. Her foot stepped on a dry twig.

The young man looked sharply around at her at the crack. He blinked. Fritha licked her lips and stepped forward quickly.

"The wizard, who died here," she said.

"Uncle Oliver?" The young man skimmed over the reeds to reach her. "You saw Uncle Oliver's death?"

Fritha swallowed. "Not only saw," she said. "He left something with me."

"The ring?" Her face must have betrayed her, for the man's anxious expression lit up radiantly. "So that's why Father can withstand him." He came within a pace of her and held out his hands. Fritha fumbled with her pouch and pulled out the ring. The young man snatched it and bolted into the air toward the fight.

Fritha's hand stinging from the quickness, she stared after him for a second. He dodged an attack and joined one of the wizards. Fritha scurried off, before the fighting could intensify. She felt light-headed with relief; the wizards might be ingrates, but the ring was gone.

Away from the fight, the mist thickened. Something rustled in the bushes ahead of her. Fritha hurried, not daring to see if it were a bird; she bit her lip as she wondered what the crow folk would do if they knew.

The village was empty, except for Bess; in the morning light, Bess's neat blonde hair shone brightly as she walked down the road. Fritha wondered what Bess was up to. No good for me, Fritha thought.

"Fritha and Bess!" called someone out of the last scraps of mist ahead of them. "That's who's missing. And I don't think they ran off to see the hermit this time."

"We did not." Bess's voice ran ahead of her. Fritha slowed down. "I saw Fritha was up to something, and followed her." The mist thinned a little, and Fritha saw Bess standing, with her hands on her hips. "I saw her giving something to one of the wizards—something she had taken from the body of the dead one."

A hiss ran about the villagers as the crow folk drew in their breaths in horror.

"How could she?" Fritha barely recognized her mother's voice. "How could she do this to us? After all we've done!"

Fritha, her blood all but congealing in her veins, walked slowly toward them. She rehearsed her excuses.

Bess turned. "And here comes the culprit herself, sneaking back to pretend nothing happened." Her delicate features contorted, her lips pulling back from her teeth. "How could you?" she snarled.

"What else could I do?" Fritha said, her voice thin.

Isobel broke in, her voice hoarse but loud, "What else? What else? Vicious little child, how could you not think of not doing it?"

Fritha tried to speak, but a rock came hurtling out of the crowd, striking her cheek. Fritha's hand rose to the blood. Her parents wrung their hands and stood back; the rest of the crow folk surged toward her.

Between one second and the next, they all changed to crows.

Fritha took to the wing. She had seen them mobbing owls far bigger than she. The crows cawed raucously and swarmed after. Ahead of her, the wizards' fight had ended. She could not scare them off by dodging too close to the fight, Fritha thought in despair; she had no recourse but to outfly them, if she could.

A crow slammed into her from behind, knocking her toward the ground. Fritha frantically fought to regain her flight, but the crows flocked around her: battering their wings and pecking, and all the time keeping up the endless din. Fritha struck the earth half way through the marsh, and the murder encircled her.

The cawing changed its note suddenly, so distinct that even half-dazed, Fritha could make it out, and the crows pulled back. Fritha lifted her head, and a hand closed around her. The murder cawed at the young wizard a little, but even their rage could be quenched by fear. His face grim, he settled Fritha in his arm and took to the air again.

I'm dreaming, thought Fritha, almost happily; it's all over and I'm dreaming. The ground swept by, below, but she felt no wind in her face. She stared down, at fields set out as squares and rectangles, at pastures dotted with tiny sheep and cows, at flocks of birds flying over a glittering river.

Suddenly, the change came again, and Fritha found herself sprawling in the wizard's arms. The wizard yelped and, unable to keep his grip, dropped her. Fritha shouted; here, she could feel the wind. The wizard plummeted after her and grabbed her arm. Fritha shouted again as he strained her bruised and bleeding shoulder, dragging her back up to his level and holding her there with one arm about her waist.

"Are you all right?" he said anxiously, his face not an inch from hers. Fritha, trying to catch her breath, could only nod. The wizard shook his head. "It's a good thing that Father wanted to thank you."

He turned his attention ahead, and his flight grew faster, the ground whipping by, until a gray castle, perched on a green mountain side dotted with cliffs, appeared ahead of them. Fritha gulped at the towers and arches; no engineering could hold that up. Then, she thought, they were wizards.

The wizard settled out in a courtyard, and the smell of baking bread rose from the building next to him. A chubby middle-aged woman, her gray hair flying about her face, bustled out of the castle. She looked at Fritha, aghast, as the wizard helped her stand, but after a second turned to him and put her hands on her hips.

"My word, Master Roland, what happened to the girl?"

Roland released Fritha. "Look after her, Tansy; I have to see my father." He swept off. Tansy muttered under her breath but ushered Fritha into the hall.

The wizards appeared again, as Tansy fussed over Fritha's injuries. Tansy scurried aside. Fritha looked up to meet Roland's father's eyes and sat up straight, putting her feet under the chair.

"She's doing well, Master Arthur," Tansy said, "but she needs to rest."

Arthur nodded. "She may rest here. Prepare her a room."

Roland snorted as Tansy bobbed her head and hurried out. "Of course she can," he muttered. Arthur's mouth tightened, and he looked at his son, but Roland looked back with bold eyes. "You wanted to offer her your gratitude. And I think it likely that her injuries are a consequence of her actions." He tilted his head to one side, looking at Fritha inquisitively. Arthur looked at her, his eyes darker but as attentive.

Fritha nodded.

Roland leaned forward. "How did that happen? All those crows were people, were they not?"

Fritha bobbed her head. "The crow folk." They watched her in silence. Her fingers twitched her skirt. "It begins with my ancestor, Simon," she said, cautiously. "He and his grandchildren came upon where bandits had killed some travelers, and looted the bodies." Silence reigned as she drew a deep breath. "One of them was the beloved son of a great wizard. In a great rage, the wizard cursed Simon and his children to be carrion crows for an hour every day, when the moon was the highest in the sky, to teach them to respect the bodies of the dead."

"That sounds like great-great-grandfather Walter," said Roland, brightly.

"Roland," said Arthur, in rebuke.

Roland looked at his father and blinked his eyes. "What, you don't think it does?" Arthur's eyes narrowed. "And his youngest son did die young and violently."

Arthur pulled back. "Not in front of commoners," he said, his voice low. Roland grimaced, and Arthur raised his hand. "Let the lass tell how what it had to do with her injuries," he said, ponderously.

Fritha licked her lips. "Well, he said it was to teach them respect for the dead, so we tried to get the curse broke by not touching the dead."

"A worthy lesson," said Arthur, his voice a deep rumble.

Fritha's voice slowed. "The wizard, your uncle..." She gestured at Roland. "He asked me to give you the ring, but died before he could give me it." She licked her lips again. "I had to take the ring from his body. When I gave you it, they discovered how I had got it, and thought the wizard would think they hadn't learned it."

Roland said, waspishly, "An unworthy lesson, if it teaches these folk to ignore the dying. If it is Walter's, it might be liftable."

Arthur snorted. "An ungenerous sort of folk. To ignore people for a dubious advantage." Fritha wondered, waspishly, if he had ever been a crow, feeling more sympathetic to Isobel than she ever had before. Arthur, oblivious to her thoughts, turned to her, and inclined his head. "We are grateful to you...." He hesitated, his face showing consternation at being unprepared.

"Fritha," she said quickly.

"Fritha. We would gladly let you recover from your injuries as a guest at our home."

Fritha bobbed her head and thanked him.

"I will have Tansy show you the way." Arthur turned to his son and said, "Roland, see to finding the book about the ring in the library."

"Library?" squeaked Fritha, before she could control herself. Arthur looked at her with pursed lips. Fritha collected herself. "I beg your pardon, sir, but there was a hermit by the swamp, that taught me my letters."

Roland's face brightened. "A most learned peasant," he said to his father, and turning back to Fritha, added, "Certainly you may read such works as you find there."

The mid-morning light filtered into the library. Fritha surveyed the titles on one shelf. She glanced about the room again, unable to keep from wondering at so many books. I ought, she thought, to look them all over before I start reading. Her heart pattered with excitement; not only had she escaped the marsh, but to such a place!

Fritha reached for a book and found herself extending a wing. After squawking in surprise, she flitted to the nearest chair to perch on its back. She had never been so surprised as this morning, she thought; the library must have driven it from her mind. She ruffled her feathers, and grumped about spending an hour waiting for minute before she resolved to make the best of it. Tilting her head to one side, Fritha contemplated the shelves; she could look at the higher titles more easily now, she concluded.

Tansy's voice thundered in the room, pulling Fritha's head up. "How did that thing get in here?" Tansy charged across the room with raised broomstick in hand. Cawing, Fritha took to the air. Tansy, her face flushed, stared after her; Fritha circled the library and settled on an upper window. Tansy scowled and called for other servants. Fritha nervously shifted her perch.

The servants came and stared; one of the men ventured off in search of a ladder; long minutes later, the librarian peered at the crow through spectacles and declared they must consult with Master Arthur. "The spells should have kept the crow out," he declared. "If they are breaking, Master Arthur must see to them."

That's good, thought Fritha; Arthur will know what is going on. She changed form again, hitting against the stone of the window frame with bruising force. The servants gaped. The man with the ladder came in, and stared with the rest, but Tansy collected her wits. "Go get her down," she ordered, "and the rest of you, you have work to do!"

The servants dispersed. A kitchen maid hesitated longer than most and, as Fritha came down the ladder said, "Like the crow in the west sitting room."

"What crow?" asked Fritha sharply, as she stepped off the last rung. The kitchen maid cringed; Tansy gave Fritha a glance like the ones she gave Arthur or Roland.

"There's a statuette," Tansy said warily, "that's of a crow. It's a magic thing, we think. Master Arthur's great-grandfather made it."

"Walter?" said Fritha, sharply. Tansy bobbed her head.

Fritha drew a deep breath, and asked to see it. Tansy led her off to see a small thing of black glass, perched among scores of trinkets. In spite of their glitter, it held her eye. Fritha licked her lips and knew what she had to look for first in the wizards' library; Walter might have written about his work.

Fritha bent over the book, straining her eyes with the tiny, crabbed writing and stiff with the hours she had spent. She turned the page once more, and read on, her eyes passing so reflexively the words nearly did not sink it. It took her a second to go back and read again, to confirm.

The change to crow overtook her, and she swept from the library, startling servants with her caws of delight, and out into the open air, where her caws echoed from the mountains. She circled the castle, stretching her wings for the hour, and flew back to the library, to make the most of her discovery.

Roland stood over the book she had been reading and frowned. Fritha flitted up as the change came, and stood beside him.

Roland looked up. "What is this?"

"Your great-great-grandfather's book," Fritha said. She smiled radiantly. "He laid the curse on my folk, and a great many others beside." Roland looked grave. "And most of them seem disproportionate to the crime, and fall on generations to come more than the criminals."

"Most unfair," Roland said.

Heartened, Fritha said, "And the charm for the curse on the crow folk is just a statuette of a crow; Tansy knew of it." She glanced at him. "Certainly I would be most grateful for the lifting of the curse."

Roland's eyebrows went up, and he took up the book. "Certainly, we must consider this." He vanished from the room, and Fritha turned to look at the shelves. Why, she thought, if Arthur lifted the curse, she could venture anywhere in the world. Humming, she looked for books about other lands.

The hour caught Fritha by surprise again, and she flitted to the back of her chair. She gave the account of the city of Mellitta a longing glance, but took to the air to fly about the castle once. Had to stretch sometime, she thought, perching on a gutter to ponder whether to circle the castle again.

"Look at them, Father!" Roland exclaimed from the nearest window. "Hundreds of curses, for generations. We can't just watch them!"

Fritha froze. She could not help but strain her ears.

"I have looked at them," Arthur said. "Good solid work, too; they have lasted this long, and all that is needed to break them is to break the charm he used."

"But, Father," said Roland, exasperated, "we can't just let the curses run. It isn't as if anyone that Walter laid a curse on is still alive."

"Some of them may be," Arthur said mildly. "Some of them were laid on wizards. We can't just lift them all; Walter may have had good reason for them."

Who let Walter decide who deserved a curse? thought Fritha.

"I will investigate them all, in order," said Roland, haughtily. Fritha cringed; the crow folk had been one of Walter's last victims.

"How is Fritha recovering?" Arthur asked.

"Well," said Roland. "She will be able to leave shortly."

"That's good," Arthur said. "I would never have let her stay here had I known how much she would disturb the servants. Why, the cook burnt a dish, the first day, because she ran off to stare at Fritha as a crow."

Fritha silently took flight again, soaring back down to the library. Who was the benefactor here? she thought mutinously. She perched on the back of the chair. The rest of the crow folk might have done nothing for the wizards, but she had—and what right had they to declare the curse, even on the rest, was right?

The change came longer before Fritha stopped fuming. She settled back down in her chair, but found the book not as engrossing as before her flight.

Fritha looked at the page again, the writing turning into black blurs. The lore it held was marvelous, but in the last day, she had lost much of her taste for reading. Her teeth closed on her lower lip; perhaps she could go back to the crow folk, the rescue by a wizard might have frightened them, she thought, but shook her head. Isobel would complain that she had not parlayed the wizards' gratitude into the lifting of the curse. Fritha sighed.

Roland walked into the room. "How are you faring, Fritha?"

Fritha turned in her chair and nodded to him. "Better," she said.

"Tansy told me you would be well soon."

Fritha let out a long breath. "She told me so this morning." Actually, she admitted to herself, I could go now.

Roland nodded and went over to the shelf to get his book. He turned back to her with it in hand. "I looked at the curses you showed me, to see if any of them are falling on the innocent," he said, heartily. "Because I must worry about William, it will take time." He shook his head. "So much work, in due time and proper order." Fritha looked at him sharply, wondering if he had decided that the crow folk were guilty. Obliviously, Roland nodded to her and left. Fritha watched him with narrowed eyes. All this pother about an act of a second: breaking the charm.

Her heart stopped for a second, and started to race, pounding in her ears. It did not need the wizards, either; she could easily break the charm herself. Fritha swallowed, looking blankly down on the book. They cared so little about the curses that it would not be hard for her to steal it.

Carefully, she put the book away; they would notice that she left it, when she was not a crow. She walked out into the corridor, trying not to glance around as if she were afraid of being seen, and took her way to the sitting room. Some of the servants glanced at her curiously, but turned back to their work as she walked by. Fritha took hold of the doorknob, thought, Lord, prosper my work, and opened the door. No one moved inside.

Fritha drew a deep breath, walked across the room, and picked up the crow. Holding it carefully in the palm of her hand, she walked down the hallway and out of the castle. A few servants greeted her; she nodded to them, and started briskly off down the mountain. She kept her ears cocked, every second, but no uproar, resulting from a discovery, followed her.

Fritha reached the nearest cliff, the wind from it chilling her and tossing her hair, and looked down at the rocks at its foot. She pitched the charm up, as far as she could throw it. It soared into the air, glittering in the afternoon sunlight, and fell again. A long minute later, Fritha heard a faint sound that must have been its breaking.

Fritha smiled. The curse was broken, and she was free and could go anywhere.

Well, except the marsh, she noted; neither her parents nor anyone else would believe that she broke the curse. Her smile deepened as she started down the mountain. So faring through the world would kill two birds with one stone, she thought merrily: seeing the world and getting away from the marsh.

Dragon's Breath

Today is cold and clear and bright;
  The frost is shining in the light.
  I smile and breathe a puff of smoke,
  Unnoticed, quite, by simple folk.
  I am old and rich; cunning and wise;
  I am a dragon in disguise.

But today, it is a dragon day
  And not a day to hide away.
  I breathe out smoke for all to see
  And know my own true ancestry.
  Just for today, I am done with lies;
  I am a dragon in disguise.

But you are breathing smoke, also:
  A secret which no one must know.
  Come, let us talk of ancient days,
  And ancient, learned, wiser ways.
  We are big of heart, though small of size;
  We both are dragons in disguise.

Never Comment On A Likeness

Sir David Markleton leaned back his chair. "Really," he drawled, "Lord Redberry—overreacted." He spread one hand; the gaslight glinted from the ruby in his ring.

Lady Goldfinch sat bolt upright in her chair, resolving to never accept another invitation from Lady Stepple. That woman sat at the head of the table, as smug as a cat that had eaten a canary. "Really," said Lady Goldfinch, frigidly. "I would have said he was foolishly generous."

Lady Stepple leaned forward. "Never speaking to her again, except on necessary public occasions?"

"If he divorced her," Lady Goldfinch said, "he would never have had to speak to her, ever." Sir David sat back and looked at her; Lady Goldfinch looked back with what she hoped was a suitably frosty expression.

Lady Stepple raised a hand. "Of course," she said, "your husband. . . ." A murmur of agreement went around the table.

Lady Goldfinch fumed. Of course Arthur would mind if she were unfaithful to him, he would have the perfect right to mind, but nothing would perturb the lords and ladies who were amused by how Lady Eastfield gave birth to a boy who exactly resembled Lord Eastfield, and how Lady Silverton raged, because Lord Eastfield was supposed to be having an affair with <u>her</u>.

"Of course, you meant it as a challenge," Sir David said. Lady Goldfinch, hating the smooth tone of his voice, looked away from him, at the reflections in the windows. "What grounds would Lord Goldfinch have for complaint? You have given him an heir, and a spare, and a third son beside."

Lady Goldfinch stiffened, not dignifying that with an answer. Even if she were to be unfaithful, she would not want this notorious gallant.

Sir David came up behind her and said, his voice low, "Alexandra." His breath brushed her hair.

Lady Goldfinch whirled around, ready to box his ears, but Sir David stepped adroitly back. "No more of this, then," he said, lightly. He tilted his head to one side, the hair falling back from his slightly pointed ear. Lady Goldfinch found herself chilled by all the stories that Sir David was a changeling.

Sir David smiled. "Let us talk of other matters." He spread one hand. "The news, perhaps. Such as the story of that poor murdered baby."

Lady Goldfinch gave him an uneasy glance. "The case last month?" she said. "The child burned to death by servants convinced it was a changeling?" She wondered if mentioning that case were a coincidence.

Sir David smiled. "That one. They are talking of having all the servants committed as insane."

Lady Goldfinch's mouth twitched. "Because they say they knew it was a changeling? How could they know it, when the baby, in fact, was not, for it did not go flying up the chimney?"

Sir David's smile deepened, unpleasantly. "Of course," he said, "the Good Folk might well have been involved—even though the baby was not a changeling."

Lady Goldfinch blinked in bewilderment.

"They are, after all, masters of glamor."

Lady Goldfinch recoiled. "'Could make a lady seem a knight,'" she thought,

"'A nutshell seem a gilded barge
A sheeling seem a palace large
And youth seem age and age seem youth,

All was delusion, nought was truth.'"

"Even so," said Sir David, like a schoolmaster to a student who had outdone himself. Lady Goldfinch flinched, realizing she had spoken aloud. "The Good Folk might have been playing with the servants. . . ."

"Then," said Lady Goldfinch, her voice like flint, "they are not good." She stared at him a minute longer, resolving that if he took a step toward her, she would box his ears. When he did not, she walked to the door.

The nurserymaid hovered by the door. Lady Goldfinch looked down at her youngest son as he fretted; even by the lamplight, she could see how flushed his cheeks were. "Perhaps I should summon the doctor," she murmured. She leaned over the baby. Edward opened his eyes. Lady Goldfinch froze. Edward had had gray eyes, like Arthur's. Now, he did not, nor did he have her own blue, but dark brown. Lady Goldfinch gulped. She had seen too much of Sir David Markleton's eyes not to recognize them in her son's face.

The nurserymaid peered into the cradle with dark eyes. "I don't think any doctor's going to know how to physic this," Jane said, darkly. She shook her head, her gray-brown hair shifting around her face. "The Good Folk have come and gone."

Lady Goldfinch gulped and straightened. After Sir David's hinted threats, she believed that. She looked back down—at the baby, she supposed. He kicked his legs and yelled. Lady Goldfinch's mouth twisted. They did say that changelings were old—just diminutive, or enchanted. She rested her hand on the cradle. Sir David told her that story to make her doubt what had happened, she knew, but the servants had believed the child a changeling. She closed her eyes.

"They do say," said Jane, "that the best way to deal with changelings is to toss them on the fire."

"No!" Lady Goldfinch whirled around. A startled yelp came from the cradle, and Jane cringed. Lady Goldfinch drew a deep breath. "We will not. Only a month ago some servants murdered a child that way." Jane tried to meet her eyes, and Lady Goldfinch added, "Do you want to join them in jail?"

Jane shook her head, pulling back. Lady Goldfinch looked into the cradle again. "For that matter, perhaps the Good Folk have bewitched him." Her hand tightened on the wood as she considered. "There are ways of detecting changelings besides the fire, and ways of breaking fairy charms." She swallowed. "We shall try some of them."

Young Arthur and his brother Theodore raced across the lawn. Lady Goldfinch stood at the window and watched them. Behind her, the baby fussed, but she did not turn back. He was growing no worse, but he looked more like Sir David every hour. Jane was smuggling the broken eggshells of the last charm out of the nursery, and they were out of charms. She shivered. Arthur would think he knew what those looks meant, and she could not bring herself to think he would wrong to do so.

Lady Goldfinch turned back to the cradle. The Englishwomen would doubtlessly blame her being an American for her over-involvement in her children. She looked down at the baby. Then, those Englishwomen would sent their daughters out into society with the advice to "never comment on a likeness." They would not find Sir David's pursuit so depraved—and they would never believe that the baby's looks were the Good Folk's fault, and not her own accident.

Her mouth compressed as she wished she had listened to the stories about Sir David more closely. Sir David was a changeling,

Sir David got the Good Folk to help him in his amorous affairs—but the rumors could not know, she reminded herself. She swallowed. Why, she did not even know for certain that Sir David was a changeling, any more than she knew Edward had been changed.

"My lady?" A maid called up the stairs. "My lady, Sir David Markleton is here." Lady Goldfinch froze. He would make her an offer, she thought in revulsion. After a second, the servant said, "Shall I tell him you are not at home?"

"No!" Lady Goldfinch called. After a second, she added, her voice calmer, "No, I shall receive him." She started down the stairs, smoothing out her skirt with one hand. She knew what he was calling about, she thought, but she could not cringe and avoid him. Her mouth tightened. Below, she saw the butler ushering Sir David into a sitting room. The fire within burned low on the hearth; Lady Goldfinch's mouth twisted as she wished she could throw him on the fire.

She stopped in the middle of taking another step. Sir David would never admit that the Good Folk had taken Edward, and not lose his bargaining chip, she thought, but he might admit some other things. A smile tugged at her mouth. She hurried down the stairs and into her husband's study.

"Sir David," Lady Goldfish said, her voice cool and smooth.

Sir David, from his seat beside the fire, leapt to his feet. "Lady Goldfinch." He inclined his head. "I hope your children are well?"

Lady Goldfinch stiffened a little, but managed to keep her voice calm. "I fear the Good Folk have harmed the youngest."

Sir David blinked at this forthrightness, but recovered quickly. "How distressing." He glanced at her sideways. "I could wish to help you, but what little I can do I commonly do for—dear friends of mine."

Lady Goldfinch drew a deep breath and tried to keep her heart from racing; a vain effort, when she knew this was the moment. "I doubt it," she said. "I think you are but taking advantage of their tricks for tricks of your own."

Sir David reared back, his eyes dilating with shock. "My lady!"

Lady Goldfinch raised her eyebrows. "Why would the Good Folk do anything for you?"

"Why, Lady Goldfinch, surely you have heard the rumor?"

"Do you think I am such a fool as to believe every rumor?" Lady Goldfinch took a step closer to him.

Sir David drew himself up to his full height. "This one is true," he said, regally.

"That you are a changeling?" Lady Goldfinch pressed.

Sir David nodded. "Yes."

Lady Goldfinch nodded. She pulled out the gun she had taken from the study.

Sir David blanched and took a step back.

Her mouth twitched. "I intend to treat you like a changeling: to throw you in the fire." Sir David glanced at the blaze, only inches behind him. "I doubt even your circles would accept a man who went flying up the chimney." Sir David's eyes narrowed. "Rumor is one thing." Lady Goldfinch's free hand swept the fire. "That is another."

Sir David drew himself up to his full height, but before he could speak, Lady Goldfinch cut in, "If the Good Folk have enchanted Edward, have them disenchant him. If they had took him, have them bring him back and take their changeling." Sir David opened his mouth. "Now, Sir David. Or I throw you on the fire and take my chances."

The sunlight shone over the sitting room, and Edward crowed on his father's knees.

"What a fine fellow he is," said his grandmother. The dowager glanced at Lady Goldfinch. "And so like his father."

Lady Goldfinch smiled. "Very like indeed."

Lord Goldfinch chucked Edward under the chin. "These things are tricky," he said, solemnly. "Babies often change." He handed Edward back to the nanny and turned to his wife as the nanny left. "Alexandra, I have heard that Sir David Markleton has decided to break off the acquaintance."

"I'm afraid it's true, Arthur," she said, a little hesitantly, and wondered what explanation she could give. She had not thought that he might be a useful sort of fellow when she made her threats.

Lord Goldfinch smiled. "Just as well. An unscrupulous fellow."

Lady Goldfinch smiled radiantly. "I do not think we will miss him at all."

The Drunken Mermaids

Morning came, despite the storm, but Colin knew it only from the light slowly increasing. He ached from clinging to the rock, his sodden clothing was growing stiff from salt, and he was so weary that the stone felt like a pillow. The squall had subsided, but the rock was still slippery, from rain and seaweed. He tried not to think of the men who had gone down with the ship.

Despite his weariness, his parched mouth kept him awake. He tried to swallow, and the pain of that stirred him. He pushed off the rock. Without the waves battering at him, he could stand.

The islet was made of the nondescript gray stone. A ring of dreary seaweed lay about the high tide mark, and more scattered where the squall had tossed it. All about, the sunrise painted the waters delicate shades of pink, yellow, and orange; only the faintest of breezes made it ripple. The skies above were filled with puffy clouds, like brilliantly colored angel feathers. Colin swallowed again and turned his head. The wreckage of the Golden Gull was still visible: wood piled up on the shore, and bodies among them. The cargo was visibly leaking. Wine, rum, and brandy all spilling, the wine coloring the sea red—the fishes were no doubt as drunk as lords—but he could drink some of that wine.

The wine-dark sea, thought Colin, as his limbs slowly came back to life. It was a pity that Uncle Archibald would never hear how his nephew had indeed listened.

He staggered to his feet. A moan sounded, barely audible over the faint breeze. Colin blinked and looked about. He had survived, after all; someone else might have.

Another rock shifted and proved to be a sailor in rags, his face weather-beaten and his hair salt-and-pepper. The man leaned on the nearest outcropping. It took Colin a minute to place him: Ned Edwards.

"Ned?"

The sailor looked up. He shielded his eyes with his hands. "Young Colin Fairington," he announced. Colin glanced at the rocks and took a step toward him, but Ned managed to walk without his aid. "A midshipman, on his first sea voyage."

Colin wondered if the sailor had been hit on the head during the wreck.

"Listen to an old salt, young Master Fairington: stick to me like glue, 'cause we're each other's proof that we aren't pirates."

Ned babbled on, about how the pirates so often marooned unpopular captains or sailors who violated their articles, that they were called marooners, but Colin took in little more than every third word. He scanned the horizon. The colors were still vivid and delicate, and uninterrupted by any sign of ships. He scowled.

"We should see if we can fetch some wine from the wreck," he said. "Or maybe even water, which would be better." Ned peered at him. "And then we could set some of the wreckage ablaze, as a signal."

Ned cackled with laughter. "You don't 'magine that any ship's sailing near enough to see it—or you wouldn't 'magine if you weren't a young pup with no sense. They ain't sailing near these rocks." He gestured about.

"Well, then," said Colin, "we aren't going to be taken for pirates, are we?"

Ned gave him a sour look.

As if anyone *would* take us for pirates with a shipwreck beside us, though Colin, but quarreling would not wet his throat. He headed down to the wreck. The sea had tossed up a wine barrel. It lay in a sandy nook and leaked about the spigot. Colin held out his hands to catch the wine and drank it down. It seemed to not reach his stomach, but be drawn into his parched mouth. It also seemed to restore his wits: he turned on the spigot and drank from it, splashing the sand with red.

The wood lay piled up, higgledy-piggledy. Colin stood in the shade of it and looked at the barrels behind the beams. The waves had carried away the food and the water, but not all of the ship's cargo.

Four hands might shift those beams, thought Colin, but he had more wine—the weakest vintage he could find—than he could readily move as it was. He should get the barrels higher on the islet before the tide came in.

Picking his way out through the stone, he came upon a smaller barrel: brandy. He looked at it a moment, remembering Christmas dinners with lighted brandy, and took up the barrel under his arm.

He emerged. The sea gulls leapt up, screaming wildly, from the bodies they had been pecking at. Colin shuddered and turned to the barrels. He had little else to distract him. He picked one up and headed up. As he passed the sand, he saw footprints not his, next to the barrel he had drunk from, coming to it and leading away from it.

"Conscientious little fellow, aren't you?" said Ned, as Colin lugged the first barrel onto the higher rock. "Doing your best for your masters."

Colin shrugged. "Won't make much difference to them." He grinned. "Unless the insurance finds out and declares that being drunk by a ship-wrecked sailor is *not* covered."

"They ain't gonna find out, pup," said Ned.

Colin shrugged again and went down to heave up more. He did not want to lose his evidence that he was not a pirate, he thought with a grin. The sea gulls screamed again, and the grin faded. Not to mention that he would go mad, alone with the corpses and the gulls, if Ned died of thirst.

At the last barrel of the six he would take—his arms ached as never before—he hefted it up and stopped, though it weighed in his arms. He thought he heard singing, and strange singing it was. After a moment, the wind shifted, the sound vanished, and not certain he had not imagined it, Colin plugged on, out of the wreck.

"Gotten all you're getting?" said Ned.

"For now," said Colin. "I even got cups."

Ned snorted. "Not going to do any good, pup. You go around drinking wine, you're going to end up thirsty."

"Worse than going without? I got the weakest vintage I could."

"Won't last you long."

"Well," said Colin, "you don't have to drink any. It will leave me more." He sat. "It was strange. I heard singing—"

Ned snorted. "*Potent* wine you have there, pup. You haven't even drunk any of it yet." He reached for the nearest spigot. Colin sat back against the stone. After a moment, Ned looked up from the wine cup. His expression was strange; baffled, Colin thought. "Very *potent* stuff—indeed. 'Cause I can hear 'em now."

Colin held his breath, and the sound came clearly enough. He made out one phrase's words: "Give me some time, to blow a man down." He scowled. The old sea shanty, but the voices almost sounded feminine, and the sea still bore no ships.

The voices came again, more clearly.

"Come all ye young fellows that follows the sea,

To me, way hey, blow the man down.

Now please pay attention and listen to me.

Give me some time to blow the man down."

Slowly, Colin rose to his feet. Moments later, Ned got up. He shambled after as Colin headed down to the tiny beach.

Not only the fishes were drunk.

Colin stood, his hands on his hips. Not even Ned's most cynical remarks about the potency of the wine could reach him, not when the wine-dark sea held mermaids frolicking, feminine forms and fish tails like an old salt's yarn. He swallowed. Like a yarn told by an ancient salt in his cups. No one else would venture such a tale because no one would believe him, that he had actually seen the treacherous, seductive mermaids.

The mermaids sang a sea shanty in voices that belied the stories about their sweet singing. The false notes and coarseness might be the wine, he conceded. On the other hand, as a curious handful swam over, he noted that the old salts left out other things from their stories. The mermaids were not, in fact, all slim young maidens, or even buxom women, but all the way up to crones. One wrinkled old mermaid grinned toothlessly at him. He glanced away, and his gaze fell on one of the maiden ones. She smiled, tossing her blond hair back from her naked body. Colin turned scarlet and looked away, out over the sea. Seductive—the old salts were not lying about *that*.

Seductive and treacherous, Colin reminded himself, for all that he could not steady his breathing. Fond of drowning men. For all that he could do nothing there but sit in the shade and drink wine, he ought to go back up the islet, to the rocks.

Ned hooted with mirth. "Should never have been a sailor, pup. The whores in any port will sport with you till you're that color for life!" He faced the mermaids. "Lad's on his maiden voyage!" he announced, and drew a roar of laughter.

"What's the matter, pup?" repeated a mermaid. "Though I must say you are a fine figure of a young pup." She swam out into his vision and smiled at him, flaunting her body. "All's well that ends well, that's what I always said," she said, falling back and flourishing her greenish tail.

"You don't always say that," said one, snidely, drawing Colin's attention back to the rest. Out of the corner of his eye, he saw Ned watching them avidly. Even the old sailor, used to the whores in the ports, was allured by these creatures with fish tails.

"Yesh she does," said another. She waved one pale hand in air. "Ash least—fig-ur-a-tive-ly." She beamed for pride at remembering the word. The complaining mermaid snarled, and the air rang with drunken and angry complaints rather than song.

"You're a fine one, pup," said Ned. "Can't be two men on the earth who'd turn such fine ladies to quarreling, not when they could be paying heed to him." He punched Colin lightly in the shoulder. "Live big!"

"Don't you mean, die big?" said Colin. He wondered if the other sailors had drowned in the wreck, if mermaids had—assisted some of the others along. "Didn't you get close enough to drowning last night?"

Ned, for a moment, looked serious. He took another swig from the barrel and glanced at how the sunlight glittered on the sea. "We should get some shade," he muttered, and the two sailors went up the rocks again.

Their quarrel dying down, the mermaids' voices came after them: "What shall we do with a drunken sailor? What shall we do with a drunken sailor?"

And the worst of it, thought Colin, was that they were not mocking him and Ned; they were just amusing themselves. He closed his eyes from a moment. He suspected that he knew why the sailors claimed that men would throw themselves into the waves after a singing mermaid.

Ned took a deep swig of wine as soon as they reached the barrels. "I suppose you'll be talking about a raft next."

Colin gave the wreck a wary glance. It might be possible at that, to get enough wood and fix it together.

Ned cackled with laughter. "No currents, pup, not that would drag you somewhere. And you're not going to rig some sails—the cloth is gone."

Oars, thought Colin, but Ned went on. "And that's without reckoning on *them*. They don't want you to leave, and a raft's going to be easy for them." He took another cup full of wine. "Nah, nothing for us but this island or *them*." He scowled as he lifted his cup.

Colin fetched himself a cup without meeting Ned's gaze.

The rocks offered little shade, and Ned drank steadily as the tide rose and fell again. Colin sat a rock over, drinking less, but his mouth would not permit him to abstain. He wished he could have found water. The mermaids sang on and on, with none of the charm that the old salts' tale spoke of. More wine seeped out of the wreck as the waves bore the first of it away.

The sunset turned the ocean and sky into a fiery tapestry. Colin sighed. After all the work, he was bone-weary, and the rock felt comfortable, once again. He closed his eyes.

Ned slammed down the cup. Colin opened his eyes with a start, but the old salt did not glance at him. His gaze was on the waters of the wreck, where the mermaids were singing.

"My clothes are all in pawn,
Go down you blood red roses, go down."

"I've had it, pup," Ned announced. "I'm going to die *big*."

Colin tried to blink his sleep away, but his befuddled mind had barely managed to take in Ned's declaration before the sailor was heading down to the sands.

"Go down you blood red roses, go down
Oh you pinks and posies
Go down you blood red roses, go down."

Colin sat up, to see Ned silhouetted against the sunset, and calling to the mermaids. "All you fine ladies, I have—resist-ed your charms too long." He spread his arms. "I ha' come to—uncondish-onally surrender."

Giggles spread from the waters. He's drunk, thought Colin. He ran as Ned waded into the water, but when Colin reached the shore, two smiling mermaids had Ned, one by each arm. One pressed her naked body against him, eliciting a broad grin from the sailor, while the other eased off his shirt and reached for his belt. The other mermaids swarmed around, smiling. Several glanced at Colin, with beguiling sweetness in their faces, and as Ned, naked, was steered to deeper water, the youngest and most innocent looking—the one who had thrown back her hair for him that morning—extended her arms.

Drowning would be quicker than hunger, came his first thought, and the second thought said, Ned looked pleased with his reception. Colin bolted up the islet. A mermaid's voice came melodiously after him, "Farewell and adieu to you, Spanish ladies," and Colin shuddered. The mermaids, and Ned, laughed, and the songs continued to chase him: "From Ushant to Scilly is thirty-five leagues!"

Colin closed his eyes, but the writhing bodies formed just as clearly in his memory as before his eyes. He groaned.

After a long night on a rocky bed, with dreams to make him blush, Colin sat on the shore. A new body floated, deep in the waters.

"So much for proof that I am not a pirate," he said, but even that piece of wit did not manage to raise his gloom.

The mermaids again sang of what to do with a drunken sailor and cast sidelong, admiring glances at him. Colin looked at the wood from the Golden Gull, up on the rocks, and wondered if it *were* possible to make a raft of it, whatever Ned said. He might be able to paddle to where a ship might find him. He walked off the beach. If the mermaids drowned him then, at least it would be while trying to escape and not in a drunken surrender.

Another quarrel broke out behind him, of who had driven him off, and who had let him escape the evening before. In spite of everything, Colin smiled.

The raft progressed steadily enough that by noon, Colin wondered whether the currents would lead him anywhere useful, or if he could just die of thirst on the raft as well as on the islet. The mermaids had abandoned their quarrels and sang once again of blowing a man down.

The waters began to heave, as if the ocean itself were boiling. Drunk though they were, the mermaids stopped singing. Some even looked frightened and pulled back toward the shore.

Slowly, a head rose above the water: a regal woman, her black hair streaming down like a wave. Though she was as naked as the other mermaids otherwise, a crown of gold and pearls rested on her head. She rose up to contemplate her subjects. One mermaid dipped her head and murmured, "Your Most Oceanic Majesty," and the others hurried to imitate her.

"Do you think you can thus set aside the report I have had of you?" She lunged forward, and the wave that followed was much larger than it should have been for a motion like that. Colin stepped back, quickly. The water lapped where he had stood; with this many mermaids about, he did not want to get in the ocean at all.

The Queen of the Mermaids did not seem to notice. Her gaze was only on her subjects. "Quarrels! Should I expect civil war to break out in my realm next? The entire ocean has rung with your squabbles! And as for your singing. . . ." She sniffed. "I could declaim your allegiance, for no true mermaid sings so dreadfully, and you are making us the laughingstock of all beneath the waves."

The Queen of the Mermaids, thought Colin, must control much of the sea. Even if only the mermaids obey her, she would be powerful.

"Shorry," said one mermaid. The others looked away from the queen.

"As for your manners—I have seen every one of you in court. You have no excuse for your ignorance!"

"They're drunk," said Colin.

The queen looked at him, her eyes narrowing. Colin explained about the cargo. She looked at the wreck, drawing slightly farther away from it. "It is of limited size," she murmured, scarcely louder than the lapping waves. "It will stop spilling in time."

"I have more," said Colin. "I can make it go on spilling wine for a long, long time."

The queen's face contorted. "What have *we* done to you?"

Murdered my proof I was not a pirate, Colin thought, with dark humor—but Ned's being a fool did not make the mermaids less murderous. "You murdered the man with me; saving my life strikes me as only just return."

The queen glanced at the other mermaids. One said, "There was another sailor on the rock. He joined us last night."

Cascades of giggles came all around. "He was amusing," said another mermaid.

"You're amusing when you're drunk," said Colin.

The queen looked on the verge of rage. Colin met her gaze. This was no time to display any weakness. "On the other hand, I have a raft. If this evening your mermaids can draw me, on it, to Queensport, I would refrain from amusing myself."

The Queen of the Mermaids smiled. It was not a pleasant smile. Colin managed to twitch his lips in response. Whatever her plans were, the risk could not be greater than staying here.

Colin warily floated the raft from the beach. He had brought down the barrels, and the setting sun was just beginning to tint the sky with yellow, but the mermaids could declare it evening at any time. He hurried to load the barrels aboard. Two of wine, to drink, and then four of brandy, and five of whisky. The raft bore them without riding too low in the water, and Colin added another one of wine.

The sun was turning all the west to the flame, and the moon hung in the east, in the rich blue of the sky.

"We shall tow this raft to Queensport!" said one mermaid, rising up about of the waves. Colin scrambled aboard, before they disclaimed any need to bring *him*, and the mermaids burst into cascades of giggles even as they surrounded the raft to tug it to sea. All young, lissome maidens, if you could ignore the tails; perhaps the older ones would not be strong enough.

One thing about the barrels, Colin thought. They shielded him enough from the mermaids' seductive forms that he could remember their habits of drowning their lovers. He wriggled to the midst of the barrels.

He could almost hear the shrug in one mermaid's voice, "To Queensport."

Moonlight gleamed over the gentle swells, making a pattern of black and silver. Colin braced himself on the raft. He had labored all day to build that raft, but he could not sleep, not yet, not when the Queen of the Mermaids had smiled as she had, when he had offered his bargain. He had to sit up; if he lay down, he would sleep at once.

Then the ocean calmed about him, all the swells sinking to stillness. Colin was not surprised, even when all the mermaids let go. Their giggles were softer than whispers, but the sea was calm enough for him to hear. He reached out to take a barrel of brandy and put his hand about the spigot.

The Queen of the Mermaids smiled at him, not an arm's reach from the raft. "I think this will suffice. You should be wary of making offers to queens, young pup."

"Do you know what this is?" said Colin. He held out the barrel, and her smile faded away. "This is brandy. It is to wine as wine is to water. If I spill it now, you will be more drunk than any of your subjects. You will be the laughingstock of the ocean."

Her eyebrows drew together. All about the mermaids swam closer, looking avidly at the barrel. The queen glanced at them. Her mouth thinned as she realized they would not just swim away if he spilled it.

She looked furious. Then, her subjects had sounded furious when they quarreled in the waters about the wreck. It did not mean that they persisted in their quarrels long. He inched the barrel farther out and moderated his voice. "Come along. Ensure that your subjects do not disgrace you."

After a moment, she shrugged, as if the game was up, and gestured for her subjects to continue drawing the raft. Colin sat back. Fickle as water, you shall not excel, thought Colin, wryly.

The sky showed the faintest traces of gray in the black. The air took on the scents of flotsam and jetsam decaying on the beach, and plants. Colin felt, vaguely, the raft grinding ashore and heard, even less distinctly, the retreating whispers of the mermaids, but he did nothing more than lay his head down.

Barrel of brandy's an odd pillow, he thought but could manage nothing more before he slept.

Seagulls screamed. Colin woke with a jolt, to limbs stiffer than the day after the squall, sunlight beating down on a white sand beach, a bone-dry mouth, and shouts: "You! What are you doing there?"

Colin looked over. The uniforms had him put his hands in the air even before the soldiers pointed their guns at him. Behind the soldiers, a crowd gawked, from babies in their mother's arms and little children peering beneath people's arms, to old men hobbling from their shaded seats, from ragged beggars with signs advertising their ailments to merchants in brocade, too surprised by the sight to realize the company they were in.

Not as deserted as the islet, Colin thought.

Colin knew how little likely it was for a midshipman to stand in the governor's residence, but then, the story he had to tell was strange, and the governor had received him in an office by the entrance, and not the grander rooms within. And the governor, like the rest of the island, had hoped that shipment would arrive soon.

"Mermaids," said the governor. "It couldn't have been mermaids." He gave Colin a baneful look that did not auger well for him if he insisted on his story.

They had not only given him all water—the sweet, sweet water—he could drink, they had given him a bath to wash him clean of the salt, and Colin did not much care whether the governor believed him. "I suppose I was not the best of witnesses,

Your Honor. There was only wine to drink, and I suppose I was tipsy most or all of the time."

The governor looked relieved—and then scowled.

"I would not, however, advise any man wrecked on that rock to put to sea on a raft and hope that the currents will bear him to Queensport."

The governor's scowl deepened.

No, there are not many explanations for how I escaped that islet, and none of them are plausible, thought Colin, amused. He looked innocently back at the governor. "I believe they retrieved much of the brandy and wine from the wreck. I know that many of the barrels were intact when I—left, and I told the owners so."

The governor looked as if wondering whether, after all Colin had said, he should believe such a statement.

Colin thought of the barrels on his raft, which the governor had to have heard of. He said, "The ship sailed into harbor this morning. The captain looked pleased."

At that comment, the governor looked relieved. Colin tried to keep his face steady. The mermaids were not the only ones to lose their judgment over wine.

Free Passage

Chloe perched by the prow of the ship and looked at the cliff ahead of them. The yellow sandstone, dotted here and there with grayish bushes, loomed over the narrowing strait. The warm wind tugged on her black hair and filled the sails behind her, bearing them through the narrow entrance to the sea beyond. The sun glinted off the sea and, up on the cliff, off metal.

Petros came up behind her. "So," he said, his voice unusually deep, "the Amazons have seen us."

Chloe looked over her shoulder at her brother. The black-haired man stared at cliff with dark eyes. "Did you think we could get by without their noticing?"

Her brother spread his hands. "Hoped." He grimaced. "The Amazons are an excellent guard for the herb."

Chloe's eyes darkened; they had no choice, she knew, only the herb could break the blight, and her father had no one else to fetch it whom he trusted not to hold it hostage. "I think, we've seen enough excellent guards already." She looked past him, to the men behind: several dozen young warriors of the Crimson Isles, their dark heads bent over their work, but when they had started out, they had had a couple dozen more. She scowled in thought.

"The Amazons are not mermecoleons, or that dreadful leopard," she said after a minute. "We could ask the Amazons for free passage."

Petros grimaced. "Their queen *might* grant it."

"What were you planning to do instead?" Chloe asked. "The Anazons outnumber us. Badly."

Light flashed from the cliff again; a pattern that could not be accidental, Chloe thought. She swallowed. Petros nodded. "We'll try it." He stepped back and called, "Markos!"

Chloe ignored the renewed bustle behind her; they had brought her to find and harvest the magical herb, not to take care for the journey. The boat slowly advanced, and the cliff flowed by, sinking down to the level of the water. A narrow valley touched the shore; on each side of the beach, the stony slopes swarmed with the Amazons, sunlight glinting from their spears and shields. Chloe gulped. She could see a fortified city, deep in the valley, but her eyes kept coming back to the rocks.

Markos appeared beside her. "My lady, you should get back."

Petros's voice carried over the ship. "No, Markos, she should stay." He strode forward. "The Amazons know that our women are not warriors; Chloe might make them wonder." He looked at his sister. "In fact, Chloe, you should ask the queen for passage."

Chloe flinched. Her eyes went back to the Amazons. Who would know she was not a warrior, she reminded herself; Petros was right there.

Show them that you are a princess of the Crimson Isles, she thought fiercely. She rose her feet, her hand smoothing out the skirt of her saffron chiton, and resisted the impulse to clench the fabric. The ship slowly approached the beach, until it came within a spear's cast.

Spears bristled from the rocks ahead of them. "Halt!" bellowed a voice. Behind Chloe, the men hurried about the sails, and the ship stopped. The waters lapped against the hull. The tall, dark-haired women watched them without moving.

"No outlander may come to the land of the Amazons," said the same harsh voice. "Go back!"

Chloe swallowed and raised her voice. "We are not coming to the land of the Amazons," she said, her voice lighter than she had hoped. She plowed on. "We are but passing by."

A stir went through the crowd—perhaps for her words, perhaps for her sex—but died quickly.

"We grant no passage," said the voice. Chloe picked out the woman, whose weathered face held the marks of years, and turned toward her.

"Your queen can," she said. "Let us ask her."

"Go back!" said another voice, younger and harsher. "Take your impudence with you!" Chloe looked toward that speaker and tried to marshal another argument when the Amazon spoke again. "Why should the queen listen to you?"

"Because the gods hate those who despise petitioners," said Chloe, formally. "Who shed blood without reason and hate justice." She stopped and hoped she had not sounded glib.

The first woman to speak turned to the second and said something; her words did not carry over the water, but her angry tone did. The second retorted, but Chloe could only make out a few words, "The ogre of the north," and "candidate." The waves lapped against the boat. Chloe licked her lips.

A long time later, the first woman turned back to the water. "We will bring your petition to Queen Helen." The second woman looked at the boat with a malevolent expression. Chloe felt too relieved to care. The first woman said, "Pull your boat up on the beach and wait."

Petros called out the orders. Chloe sat, her heart pounding; she still had to speak to the queen. The boat lurched into movement. Chloe forced herself to take a deep breath. You are a princess, she reminded herself.

The city swarmed like an anthill as the ship drove into the shore, and as they waited. We mean them no harm, Chloe reminded herself; why should they not let us pass?

The sun inched higher. Out of the city came a party, and in its middle stood a woman on whose dark hair gold flashed. Chloe gulped and clambered out of the ship to stand on the

sands. Petros came after her, with three other men, but Chloe
looked only at the approaching queen.

The Amazons formed a line before them, a spear's cast away,
and watched the outlanders with wary dark eyes. A tall woman
of middle years, a golden circlet on her black hair, stood in their
center and looked at Chloe.

"Who are you, who claim to be passing by our lands?" Queen
Helen said, her voice ringing.

"I am Princess Chloe, of the Crimson Isles," Chloe said,
pleasantly surprising herself with the strength of her voice. "The
crops of the isles are blighted, and to break the curse, we need a
herb of Serpent Islands." She gestured up the strait. "In that
sea." Queen Helen looked considering. Chloe lowered her arm.
"We want nothing more than to go there, and to return by this
strait. We mean you no harm; indeed, we will do nothing to
you."

Queen Helen's mouth pursed. "And if I refuse you?"

Chloe felt her tongue freeze. Petros took a step forward. "My
father the king told me to bear my sister on this quest." He met
the queen's eyes. "It would be my duty to try to go on." He
looked about. The queen's escort, Chloe noted, was larger than
the ship's company, but not much.

Queen Helen smiled a little at this impudent half-threat.
"Stay here," she said. Lowering her voice, she spoke to a woman
beside her, and a dozen Amazons fell back to hold council.

A few grains of sand had worked their way into Chloe's
sandal, where they ground against her foot as she waited; she
wished she dared to pull off the sandal and shake them out. The
Amazons on guard shifted a little. One of Petros's men eyed the
nearest Amazon, and the woman looked back at him with bold
eyes. Chloe remembered how the Amazons kept up their
numbers, and looked sharply away.

Up on the rocks, just out of a spear's range, more Amazons
stood. The rocks half-hid them, but Chloe picked out two

companies, one creeping slowly closer. Behind her, she heard the men on shipboard surreptitiously readying their weapons, but Petros stood like stone next to her. Chloe wondered how he managed it.

A woman sprang from the Amazons coming toward them and ran to the other group among the rocks. Chloe bit her lip. A messenger? she thought.

Queen Helen's voice rose again. "I have decided!" The woman stalked like a lioness across the sands. She stepped past the band of warriors and spoke in a lower voice, her tone formal. "Princess Chloe, take your ship, and go onward. You may pass by our lands now, and to return."

Chloe's shoulders slumped, and she let out a long breath.

A voice rang from the rocks: "Treachery!" An arrow whistled through the air within an inch of Petros.

"Your warriors!" Chloe called to the queen, panicking. The queen looked shocked but could do no more before a volley of arrows flew after the first one. Chloe fell back to huddle beside the boat. The Amazons swarmed out of the rocks—she had not realized how close they were—and Petros's men pushed by her, weapons in hand. Blood flowed, and the queen's guard moved to the defense of their comrades.

"Stop this!" Helen's voice barely carried over the din, and Chloe knew that she heard it only because she was not caught up in the battle. Crouched against the hull, she saw the queen rise up, gesturing with her weaponless hands. An arrow flew through the air, and into the queen's throat. Chloe could not move.

"You have murdered your queen!" shouted one of the Amazons. "Fall back!" Some of the Amazons started to, and Petros shouted, "Men of the Crimson Isles, to the ship!"

In a minute, Chloe knew not how, the combatants had parted, and the beach lay empty except for the corpses—over a dozen of those. Chloe gulped. Near her feet lay the young man who had been eying the Amazon. Chloe's eyes drifted over the beach. Where the queen's guard had stood lay that Amazon, her eyes staring sightless at the sky. The air seemed suddenly darker, and Chloe, woozy, grabbed the hull and closed her eyes.

"Chloe!" said Petros. "Are you hurt?"

Chloe opened her eyes for a second and closed them again. She shook her head. "What happened?" she said, weakly.

"I wish I knew," Petros said grimly. He looked over the sands to the queen's body. "I do not think it safe to leave, whatever the queen said."

Chloe gulped, thinking that staying might be safer, but it was not safe. She opened her eyes. On the other side of the beach the Amazons gathered. Two of them disputed bitterly. Their words did not carry on the breeze, but she watched their angry gestures, and wondered what authority they held. Chloe licked her lips; one of them was the second woman who had ordered them off, who had arguing they could not petition the queen.

After a minute, the other woman made a gesture of concession, and stalked toward the ship, coming not as near as Queen Helen had. "Outlanders!" she shouted. "Passage is in the hands of the queen! We have no queen! You may not pass!"

Chloe's mouth fell open.

"When we have elected our queen, you may petition her!"

Silence fell, broken only by the breeze and the lapping of the waves. Chloe's head sank. After a long minute, Petros roused himself. "Give us leave to honor our dead!"

Silence fell for a longer minute. The woman finally nodded her head. "And we will honor ours!"

The funeral pyres glowed sullen red in the evening gloom. The breeze flowed out from the land, bearing the scent of dried grass and a chill. Chloe shivered. We meant them no harm, she thought.

The Amazons stood guard on their pyres and gave the men the wary glances they had when they first gathered up their dead. Chloe turned away and walked to the ship. Petros looked up from talking with Markos as she approached.

"Any movement from the city?" he asked.

Chloe shook her head.

Markos swore. "How long does it take to elect their queen?"

"Weeks, with our luck." Petros rubbed his forehead.

Chloe crouched down by the men and lowered her voice. "If they're intent on choosing their queen, we might sneak by."

Petros's mouth twitched. "We would have to fight our way through on the way back."

"You thought of doing that both ways, or sneaking through." Chloe met his eyes. "Do you know why the Amazons attacked us?"

"They claimed," said Markos, "that we were preparing to attack and kill the queen."

"They would," said Petros, sourly. He looked over the beach and got to his feet. "First, we check for guards; they could slaughter us on the spot." He stepped out onto the shore, and Chloe scrambled after him.

A voice boomed over the sands. "What are you looking at, outlander?" A woman came out of the darkness and loomed over the pyres.

"Lady Melantha," said one of the Amazons in fright. The uncommonly tall woman gestured her not to move and glared at Petros.

Chloe pulled back, thinking this woman looked like the messenger between the two groups that had first attacked the ship, and wondering if she was imagining it. She peered at Melantha. The woman gestured, reminding Chloe of the second woman who had ordered them off, and of the one who had argued over whether the ship could leave when there was no

queen to give them leave. Chloe gulped: that would make
Melantha a woman of importance among the Amazons.

Melantha smiled a little. "I have set guards. There is no queen
to give you free passage, and you will not have it without a
queen." Her eyes narrowed. "Olympe was a fool to let you wait
to petition the new queen."

Chloe quailed. Fighting their way through was still folly, but
asking had proven no less foolish.

Sunlight beat down on the plain between the city and the beach.
The funeral pyres had burned down to ashes, and the Amazon
guards, no longer keeping a watch on the fires, kept it on the
ship. Chloe looked past them, at the two women being escorted
out of the city.

One of the guards noticed her interest. "The games," she said,
her tone belligerent. "They will show who is fit to be the queen
of the Amazons." The Amazons took up positions across the
plain.

"As if there were any question," another guard said, her voice
heavy with contempt. "Olympe is a candidate only because her
mother was queen."

Chloe looked at her. "They put her forth for the games for
that?" she asked.

The guards looked at her with disdain for her ignorance. "She
fought a monster—a little one, but a monster—and they named
her candidate for that, seven years ago."

"If her mother had not been queen," grumbled the other, "that
monster would never have been accepted. Melantha fought a
true monster, an enormous ogre; she is the only fit candidate."
The Amazon grinned. "Not only did she protect us from the
ogre, Melantha saw what you were up to, preparing to attack."

"You were sneaking up on us," Chloe said, hotly.

"She saw your preparations," said the first, "so she got us close enough to mean something."

Chloe looked from one to the other. Her heart started to pound. The Amazon went on, saying, "Close enough to stop you in your tracks, and you could even deny intending. . . ." Chloe barely heard her, as her thoughts formed: Melantha had got the Amazons to fight, and the queen had died, and now Melantha could become queen.

"Melantha saw us," Chloe said, her voice cutting through the Amazon's. "Or Melantha claimed to see us, and fomented the fight, and now she can claim a crown as her reward!" Chloe drew a deep breath. She had brought harm, no matter that she had not meant it, and the Amazons might be in danger of a wicked queen, brought about by her arrival. Her hands clenched into fists in rage.

The Amazons stepped back, looking aghast. "What did the outlander say?" said a woman further back. Chloe looked up to see Amazons all over the plain looking at her, and realized she had been shouting.

"She accused Melantha," shouted another as the rumors flew through the Amazon host, too numerous for Chloe to hear more than a buzz.

"What is this outlander doing?" Melantha shouted. "Fomenting trouble?" She raised a fist in the air. "You know our laws; no outlander is part of our counsels!"

"No outlander *man* is part of our counsels!" Olympe shouted. Melantha looked bitterly at her. Olympe drew a deep breath. "This is an outlander woman. Let her speak."

"You!" Melantha spat. "You who fought a snake and claimed yourself a candidate for the queen! Your mother killed a dragon! You are unworthy of her place!"

Olympe drew a deep breath. "My sisters! Let us hear the outlander woman! If you find her story pointless, I will withdraw my candidacy!"

Melantha stepped back, blinking. She collected herself as a murmur of assent went through the Amazons. "Let her tell her false tale, and you withdraw your candidacy!"

"Not if it is false," Olympe said, with dignity. "Only if it is pointless. We may grant her a mistake." Melantha started to speak, but Olympe cut her off. "If she is such a tale-bearer, why do you fear her?"

Melantha grimaced. Olympe turned to Chloe and gestured. "Come before us and speak."

Feeling every eye on the beach upon her, Chloe slowly walked before the two candidates. One way or another, she was about to decide the fate of the Amazons, she thought, since no one else had seen what she had, and felt cold. She raised her head. "We had spoken with Queen Helen, and she had decided to grant us passage, when Melantha called out treachery. It was Melantha who claimed to see my brother's men preparing to attack."

"Diotoma's women saw them!" shouted one woman. "Melantha came to tell us."

"We did not—you did! Melantha. . ." The Amazon's voice trailed off into silence. The wind whipped the grasses on the plain. Melantha's mouth worked.

Chloe drew a deep breath and added, quickly, before Melantha could devise a tale, "And now Melantha can become queen." Her thoughts jumped to the fight. "In fact, Queen Helen fell to an arrow shot from behind her; perhaps Melantha made sure of the death."

"You wretched child!" Melantha's face contorted. She reached for her spear. Chloe took a faltering step backward, and Olympe jumped to wrestling with the other candidate for the spear. Other Amazons ran up. Chloe took another step backward and collided with someone. Petros's hand came down to seize her elbow. "Come back," he said, grim-faced.

"Trying to run away?" shouted an Amazon.

Chloe remembered the pyres on the beach. "If you want to speak to me," she snapped, "do it at the ship. *I* did not attack one of you."

Olympe rose from the ground, her face stained with blood and dirt. At her feet, four Amazons held down the still struggling Melantha. "Let her go. We do not need her testimony to convict Melantha." Her face set in bitter lines, Olympe inclined her head to Chloe and Petros. "Go back to your ship and wait. I do not think it will be for long."

Melantha's face contorted with hatred; Chloe gulped and walked away, feeling Melantha's gaze on her back the entire walk back the ship.

At least it was over, she thought, as she reached it.

In the gray morning light, Chloe stood over the ashes. Another day. She wondered if Melantha had devised a story to cover for herself. Melantha was, after all, a candidate for the throne, and her accuser an outlander, not even a warrior.

"Hallo," shouted one of the men, waving toward the city. Half a dozen Amazons walked across the plain toward them. All about her, the men reached for their spears and shields.

"Princess Chloe!" The leader raised her hand to hail the boat. "Queen Olympe wishes you to attend her in the city."

Chloe slowly got to her feet. "Alone?" she said.

The leader's eyes went over the men. "No," she said, reluctantly. Chloe guessed that Olympe had ordered for them to permit it only if she asked. "But six men—no more."

But they had to know she would ask, Chloe thought. She turned to Petros, who nodded and picked out the five. Wind blew in from the sea, hissing over the sands and grass. The men around her, Chloe followed the Amazons over the plain. The city slowly rose up ahead of them.

On the rocks outside the city wall, Melantha's broken body sprawled, staring blankly at the sky. Dried blood splattered over the stone around her.

Chloe forced herself to her full height as she walked through the gate.

Within the gates, a straight road lead up the royal palace, and in the square before it the Amazons gathered. Olympe sat enthroned there, in robes of crimson and a golden crown.

The Amazons drew to one side as they reached the square, and Chloe stopped at its verge. "Queen Olympe."

"Princess Chloe." The queen smiled a little. "It appears in one thing you told my mother a lie." Chloe froze, her mind racing. Olympe's smile deepened. "You told her you would do nothing to the Amazons." A ripple of laughter ran through the assembly, and Chloe asked.

Olympe turned to one of her counselors and lifted up a box. "Queen Helen defeated a dragon who threatened this land, and so was named a candidate, and later the queen. It is only fitting that a piece of the dragon's treasure be bestowed on the one who saved the land from a greater peril." She lifted up a necklace of pure gold, sparkling in the light.

Chloe walked unsteadily forward to the throne. Olympe lowered the heavy, cool necklace around her neck. She straightened, feeling the burden on her shoulder blades.

"It is just as well for me that you are no Amazon," Olympe said, "or they would have named you a candidate after Melantha's trial, for dealing with the peril of *her*, and queen after."

Chloe drew a deep breath and met the queen's eyes. "Then it is just as well that I am not an Amazon, for I have my quest," she said, her voice steady. It was for that that I spoke with your mother the queen." She smiled. If there were any other strange peoples along their journey, she would insist on speaking with them; they had lost fewer men here than anywhere else.

A ripple of laughter ran through the Amazons. Olympe smiled back. "So you did. Take your free passage, now and when you return."

Publication History

Also by Mary Catelli

Curses And Wonders
Dragon Slayer
Eyes of the Sorceress
Fever and Snow
Mermaids' Song
Sword and Shadow
The Book of Bone
Witch-Prince Ways
Dragonfire and Time
Enchantments And Dragons
Jewel of the Tiger
Over the Sea, To Me
The Dragon's Cottage
The Maze, the Manor, and the Unicorn
The White Menagerie
A Diabolical Bargain
Madeleine and the Mists
Magic And Secrets
The Lion and the Library
The Princess Goes Into The Forest
The Wolf and the Ward
The Witch-Child and the Scarlet Fleet
Treachery And Spells
Winter's Curse
Crow Curse
Free Passage
Isabelle and the Siren
Journeys And Wizardry
Lifestone

Magic of the Lost God
Never Comment On A Likeness
One Name
The Drunken Mermaids
The Turtle in the Sea of Sand
Were I You
Where There Is Smoke